DEAD IN THEIR TRACKS

A MITCH KEARNS COMBAT TRACKER BOOK

JT SAWYER

Copyright February 2016 by JT Sawyer
Updated May 2021
Edited by Emily Nemchick
Cover Art by ZamajK
Jtsawyer.com

No part of this book may be transmitted in any form whether electronic, recording, mechanical, photocopying, or otherwise, without written permission of the publisher.
This is a work of fiction and the characters and events portrayed in this book are fictitious. Any similarity to actual persons, living or dead, businesses, incidents, or events is entirely coincidental and not intended by the author.

THANK YOU

Thank you for buying this book! I hope you enjoy reading it as much as I enjoyed researching and writing it.

Join my email list if you would like to receive notifications on future releases or a FREE copy of a short Mitch Kearns' story, *Blood On the Mesa* which highlights Mitch's fieldcraft skills during his FBI days as he tracks down the clues connected with a murder case in the desert near Winslow, Arizona. To receive the free story, visit jtsawyer.com

PROLOGUE

Turkmenistan

Black clouds moved across the moon overlooking the seaside estate on the leeward side of Turkmenistan off the Caspian Sea, providing cover for the woman darting along the knee-high stone wall lining the courtyard of the three-story mansion. Thick leaves accumulated on the cobblestones indicated that there had been little upkeep of the grounds, giving the outward appearance that the place was unoccupied.

Devorah Leitner's sleek figure floated across the narrow walkway that led to a side door, her MP-5 submachine gun kept at low-ready. Her handler, an older man named Anatoly, was behind her with his rifle covering the high ground on the left. A four-man team nestled in the shrubs twenty yards to the rear covered her approach and had already silently sniped the two rooftop sentries. Dev's fingers were still sore from the one-hundred-foot climb up the cliff face they had to perform to breach the estate grounds. Their Zodiac boats were tethered below and would provide their exodus back to an island seven miles away.

Dev knelt down before an oaken door and removed a set of lockpicking tools from her vest pocket, working the mechanism. She whispered over her shoulder, speaking in Hebrew. "Ten seconds."

"Once we're inside, I'll take the corridor to the right and prepare to let our men in from the other side while you head to the utility room and shut down the power," said the older man in a stern voice.

She tried to hide her irritated smirk. Dev knew the plan intimately and didn't need any reminders. She finished manipulating the lock and then slowly opened the vault-like door, its rusty hinges groaning as it moved inward. Dev flipped on her small flashlight and the two warriors proceeded inside, stepping silently on the hand-hewn stone flooring that led into the safe house.

It had been four years since she began working for Anatoly's company, Gideon, which specialized in rescuing kidnap and ransom victims. The K & R industry had burgeoned in recent years and Anatoly's former occupation as a high-level Mossad agent working for Israeli Intelligence and Special Operations had provided him with an endless list of employment opportunities from families who had exhausted the usual diplomatic routes to freeing their loved ones. In this case, they were after an American businessman who had been abducted three weeks earlier while working on negotiations between the Turkmenistan government and a U.S. corporation. At least that's what the man's family had told them. While Gideon had done its best to uncover the entire abduction story, Dev knew that hostages were often kidnapped for reasons other than mere dollars.

This was her first long-range assignment with Anatoly

and she sought only to perform her job efficiently and rescue the victim. Any thoughts of winning her handler's approval were secondary. At least that's what she tried to tell herself. Anatoly was a three-decade veteran of such high-risk black ops and she held him in utter reverence. She had perfected her skills through constant application on missions abroad but now she felt like a gymnast atop a balance beam before an immense crowd.

Dev secreted herself against the wood-paneled walls until she came to the first intersection. Peering around the left side, she saw a door twenty feet ahead. According to the crude intel they'd gathered on the estate, the circuit breaker was in a utility room across from the kitchen. The plan was to eliminate the power grid while Anatoly and his other shooters swept into the back room and secured the hostage. *This scheme sounded good on paper back in the briefing room two days ago but Murphy's Law always seems to rear its ugly head when it wants. I hope this is a hasty snatch-and-grab.*

He tapped her on the shoulder and indicated his departure down the pathway to the right. She saw him trot into the shadows and disappear. The dim passageway felt more claustrophobic now that she was alone. Clutching her weapon, Dev took a deep breath while sliding along the wall towards her objective.

Nearing the utility room door, she squelched her ear-mic once to indicate her forthcoming actions. She huffed out a sigh, irritated that there was a heavy padlock securing the entrance. Dev slung her rifle and inspected the bulky contraption. She reached into her vest for her lockpicking tools again. As she hunched over, Dev felt the cold sensation of a pistol barrel pressing into the back of her neck.

"Back up and show me your hands," said a voice in Arabic.

Dev turned and stared up at the tall figure towering over her. His thick beard obscured his face, giving him an otherworldly appearance. He waved the HK pistol at her, yelling while reaching up for the two-way radio attached to his breast pocket. Dev swiftly drove her right hand up over the top of his pistol while she sidestepped, wrenching his weapon hand back until she heard his wrist ligaments pop. He winced, releasing the pistol, but then struck her with a left cross along her cheek. Dev recoiled into the wall, dropping the HK and ducking from another incoming blow from the man's gargantuan fist. There wasn't time to grab her own weapons and she slammed him in the upper quad with her instep then backhanded him across the side of his neck.

This slowed him for a second but only enraged him further. He rushed forward in a linebacker tackle, shoving her into the wall with such force that she felt her ribs compress. Dev drove her fingers into the soft cartilage beside his trachea and then grabbed him by the hair, slamming his head down into her upcoming knee.

He shuffled back and reached into his cargo pocket for a collapsible baton then flailed it wildly at her head. His first strike connected with the side of her arm which she'd raised up to protect her ribs. As he repositioned for another swing, she rushed in before he could deliver and drove her fingers into his left eye. He shrieked and backpedaled while Dev slammed her boot into his groin followed by an elbow strike across his face. She knocked the baton from his hand with a downward hammerstrike then retrieved it and slammed the brute across his forehead with all her might. He went limp against the wall, sliding to the stone floor. *Damn, he was a beast. That should take the fight out of him for a few hours.* Though the reality of deadly combat was present in each mission, she tried to avoid it if possible and knew he no longer posed a threat.

Dev was trembling, the adrenaline pulsing through her veins as she tried to catch her breath. She rubbed her sore arm, making sure nothing was broken but feeling the dull throb where a severe contusion was forming. She took a hard swallow and scanned the hallway in either direction. Dev retrieved her lockpicking tools from the ground and then paused, glancing down at the unconscious guard. She leaned over and went through his pockets, finding a set of keys. Dev removed the suppressed Glock from her leg holster and walked back to the utility room door.

"What's happening—what is your status?" She could hear the edge in Anatoly's voice in her ear.

"Just met with some resistance. The power will be disabled shortly. Wait for my squelch."

She slowly opened the padlock and swung the door inward. The cinder-block room was lined with slate-gray metal cabinets that housed the central fuses for the building. Dev scanned the panel to locate the main terminal. After squelching her walkie-talkie three times, she flipped the red control switch. The humming of the circuit breaker box ceased and the room went dark. Moments later, the sound of flash-bang grenades and the cadence of rifle double-taps emitted from the corridor behind her. She retreated from the room, stepping over the inanimate figure on the ground, and made her way to the back room where the captive was supposed to be located.

Rounding the corner, she paused to make sure no bullets were flying in her direction. The staccato of gunfire ceased and she heard the comforting sounds of her colleagues shouting in Hebrew that the room was secure. Dev sprinted down the hallway and entered the haze of gunsmoke. The overwhelming odor of sweat and urine permeated the stagnant air and she held her sleeve up over her nose. Anatoly's men were fanned out along the room, inspecting the four dead abductors who were clad in black fatigues and bore Middle Eastern complexions.

Dev pushed through the fog of smoke, moving past a wheelchair whose leather restraints were saturated with dried blood. Her boots crunched over some broken teeth on the ground and she kicked aside a pair of tarnished pliers. As the haze dissipated through the open door, the flashlights revealed the outline of the cavernous room.

God, I hope he's still alive, Dev thought. *Though being in here with these disgusting pigs for three weeks, there may not be much of a human being remaining in him.*

With the horrific images of past victims running like a reel though her head, she knew that many hostages remained hidden from their rescuers, thinking they were another hallucination from their drug-induced stupor, or they were in such a catatonic state that any sense of hope had been purged from their traumatized psyche.

"Mr. Janson—Neal Janson—we are here to rescue you," she whispered tenderly, trying to sound non-threatening. Her flashlight scanned the furthest recesses of the chamber, past a soiled mattress to where the silhouette of a stooped figure sat.

The frail man was scrunched in a ball in the corner like part of him had melted into the fissures of the damp bricks. Dev moved up to him slowly, knowing he would either remain paralyzed from shock or he would lash out at her, thinking she was another abductor. The sounds of the other men in the room went silent in her head as she focused on the despondent figure before her. Part of his left ear was missing, the edges jagged in appearance like it had been sawed off rather than cleanly severed. Cigar burn marks dotted his neck and forearms and his anemic skin color made him stand out even in the dark recess.

She reholstered her pistol and placed her outstretched hands in front of her as she knelt a few feet before him.

"Mr. Janson, we are here to get you out. My name is Devorah. Your family sent us."

The man slightly twisted his head, his one good eye staring at her while the other remained closed from the heavy bruising which encircled his right socket. His cracked lips parted, revealing his blackened gums.

"They can't hurt you anymore," she said, pointing to the scene behind her. "We are going to get you back home. Can you walk?"

Janson nodded while tears streamed down his cheeks. He shuffled forward, resting his grimy fingers upon her knee and weeping. She held his hand and nodded back towards one of the men near the entrance.

Petra, a wiry operator, came up beside her and the two of them helped the feeble man to his feet. "We need to get some distance from this place while we can," said Petra.

Dev nodded in response and she helped walk Janson to another operator near the entrance. After the injured man was escorted out, Dev scanned the room one last time for any items of value then retraced her steps down the hallway. As she came to the intersection near the utility room, Anatoly came up beside her, giving a slight nod of disapproval.

"What?" she said, her eyebrows raised.

He moved his pistol towards the unconscious man slumped on the floor. Anatoly fired a round into the large figure's head, spraying the concrete floor a wine color.

"I told you before, we don't leave loose ends—someone that can possibly put a face to our work."

"He went down hard—I saw to it. He wouldn't have come to for a long time."

Anatoly shook his head, lowering his pistol. "This is why there is a sliver of doubt in me—doubt that you can take the reins of my company one day."

"I've passed all of your training, exceeding even some of the former Mossad operatives you have. Just because I won't execute someone—that man couldn't have even made out our faces in here, it's so dark."

"There is no margin for error."

They turned to walk away and she grabbed his arm. "You don't treat the others who work for you with nearly the same scrutiny. I asked you long ago to see me as just another one of your staff—without any special treatment."

The man placed his weathered hand up to her face, brushing a lock of black hair off her cheek. "You, Devorah—you bring me so much joy and so much worry—my daughter."

1

SEVEN MONTHS Later

CASA GRANDE, Arizona

FBI AGENT MITCH KEARNS was finishing teaching the last segment of a three-day fieldcourse in mantracking to law-enforcement personnel in the desert training facility used by the Casa Grande Police Department south of Phoenix. It had been a sweltering weekend of advanced training in reading field signs, deciphering crime scene footprints, and pursuing the instructors over rugged terrain.

Mitch had learned his trade initially growing up on a ranch in southern Arizona. Later, as a combat tracker in the 1st Special Forces, he refined his tracking skills in Afghanistan and Africa on a daily basis running counter-insurgency operations. Now, he relished time in the field, especially working with other agencies. He always leapt at the opportunity to teach and had an utter disdain for office work. This had kept him from rising up through the ranks during his six years on the FBI's hostage-rescue team (HRT) and he was content to stay in field operations.

The crow's feet around his eyes were pronounced for someone who was only thirty-four, and he looked ten years older, with the heavy stress lines etched into his face. Some of that was caused by a lifetime in the elements, the rest was the residue that came from his scorched soul. He was burnt out, a spent cartridge. The effects of eight years of combat missions had eroded away the sleeve on his humanity. He had joined the FBI on a friend's referral but he had no love of the job other than when he was tracking fugitives in the field or teaching. Mitch easily passed the qualifications and exams for entry, his background in special operations having allowed him to progress to his present position.

However, Mitch clung to a black-and-white moral code that didn't mesh well with the modern world. He'd accepted the job because the work was familiar but he had a hard time swallowing the civilian justice system which often found the accused embroiled for years in court battles ending in a sentence that hardly reflected the crime, something that, a century earlier, would have been dealt with at the end of a braided rawhide rope swinging from a cottonwood tree in some lonely canyon.

It seemed like every agency training session was about new safety protocols, fugitives' rights, Homeland Security regulations, or federal budget constraints. The rules of engagement had changed and he thought he knew what it must have been like for the cowboys of old once cars entered the western landscape. Mitch often got write-ups at work about his appearance, which usually consisted of a five-day scruff and non-regulation cowboy boots. However, his exemplary conduct in the field had caused his supervisors to provide some leniency.

Though his career choices had meant a chaotic lifestyle, often working absurd shifts in all manner of conditions, the last thing he wanted at present was any kind of drastic change. His daily regime in both his personal and professional life was rigidly maintained. He sought to control every aspect of his world down to the tiniest detail, even to the extent of having the timer on his toaster at home calibrated so his morning breakfast of waffles was perfectly browned in one minute, twenty-seven seconds.

Though he had always been a stickler for detail, his life had been less restrictive prior to a year ago on a dreadful day in November when his wife of eleven years filed for a divorce. Too much time deployed or spent on field assignments had whittled away their fragile relationship. When he had finally committed to spending more time at home, they both found that their lives had become so separate over the years that there was little that they had left in common. Mitch was eager to work things out but Becky needed more stability and fewer broken promises. The dissolution was done without dispute but Mitch felt like the fabric of his world had been permanently torn, his life spiraling out of control. He poured himself into his work, taking on more training assignments and extra shifts or filling in at his friend's ranch on the city limits where he currently resided.

Mitch hovered over the three-man tracking team and observed their progress during the final culmination exercise. His eyes narrowed as he examined the faint boot prints in the sand that his co-instructor, Perry Kovac, had laid down earlier.

"You've picked up all the signs during the last mile of tracking but there's one thing you may have overlooked," he said, squatting down beside the three police officers whose dusty gear bore testament to the last few days in the backcountry. The men scrutinized the trail through the sand and cacti that they had just spent the morning covering then they discussed the visual evidence they'd catalogued. Each of them looked at Mitch with puzzled expressions.

Mitch tilted his chin up, sniffing at the air. "Notice anything?"

The men followed in unison, inhaling the scents coming off the creosote bushes and mesquite trees. The youngest officer craned his head towards the nearest overhanging mesquite branch. "Something smells putrid—it's very faint but it's there."

"Excellent. I took some sardines and smeared a little on the branch above your head." Mitch stood up, the sun backlighting his wiry six-foot-two frame. "Remember to use all of your senses when tracking a fugitive, not just what your eyes can locate. Your life may depend on it one day. If a subject is a smoker, has a particular ethnic diet, has spent the night around a campfire, or just has the B.O. of a road-killed badger, then it can tip you off to their presence where no tracks can otherwise be found."

Mitch put his fingers up to his lips and emitted a high-pitched whistle to alert the other teams to regroup at his location. When the rest of the tracking students arrived, he reiterated the lesson in scent awareness to the twelve other men and women. While he finished his summary of the weekend's topics, Perry came up alongside him with a handful of course certificates as they all squatted under the shade of some nearby Palo Verde trees. After the training wrapped up, the instructors gave hearty handshakes to each member and then began packing up their teaching materials.

Mitch and Perry had known each other for the past two years while working at the FBI's Phoenix Division. Mitch had begun there shortly after joining the bureau and his hard-won combat experience was quickly put to use on HRT and joint U.S./Mexico operations. Perry had worked as an undercover narcotics cop in El Paso, Texas before transferring to the FBI. Perry decided a relocation north would be a good career move to start over away from the seedy border towns he frequented in his line of work. Both men were skilled trackers but Mitch was the more seasoned field operator, always spending time in the wilds on his days off or volunteering with search-and-rescue.

Where Mitch was content to ride out the next few years in his current role in the field, Perry's ambition was to become regional director of all the bureaus in the Southwest.

"You headed back to the office or home?" said Perry.

"Home for sure. I've been going at it now for nine days straight and just want to lie in the hammock out back for a day or two. What about you?"

"I'm in the doghouse right now with my wife. She thinks there's something goin' on between me and the office manager on the first floor—you know, Rachel."

Mitch raised his eyebrows. "Well, is there?"

Perry shrugged his shoulders, emitting a slight grin. "Look, it's not like I'm a player. Rachel and I hooked up one time when the old lady was out of town."

"Dude, what the hell? You're married to a lovely woman and you're screwing around behind her back. That's just bad karma that's gonna smack you in the face some day."

"It was one time, bro. It's not like it's going to happen again. Besides, we can't all be monks like you." Perry patted him on the shoulder. "And what's this 'karma' shit—you going New Age on me?"

Mitch sighed and ran his hand along the back of his neck, wanting to change the subject. He had heard a few rumors about Perry's after-hours interests from other colleagues but it never interfered with his conduct on the job so he disregarded it.

"Heard anything about the bureau chief job in Phoenix yet?" Mitch said.

"It's still on the backburner. Nothing's opened up—not with this new interim chief in from the East Coast. This is my third attempt and I'm getting pretty restless—read *pissed off*—about all the red tape.

"Yeah, Evan Ryker—he's a real dilettante. Prefers to interact with his staff via the keyboard rather than in person. I think I've spoken with the dude three times in the past month and yet he walks by my desk every time I'm at the office. Plus, I don't have much to say about a guy who wants more funds allocated for the cyber division than for field agents."

"Ah, men like us, and especially you, are fucking dinosaurs, bro. One day soon, we'll be replaced by drones."

"There's never going to be a substitute for sweaty grunts on the ground."

"Speak for yourself, man. I showered this morning and put on deodorant. You're the one who kept the female students at bay."

Mitch chuckled. "A man oughta smell like a man." He nodded at Perry as they headed towards their vehicles. Mitch tossed his gear bag in the back of his weathered jeep and did a final sweep of the shade structure where they had conducted the lecture portions of the course.

The men bid farewell and drove off in their respective

directions. Since his divorce, Mitch had taken up residence in an old bunkhouse on a friend's ranch on the cusp of the city limits. It was a small cattle operation north of Phoenix and had the rustic feel of the place he had grown up at while only being a forty-minute drive to work. With all of the ranch hands attending a rodeo in Prescott, Mitch would have the place to himself. *No emails, no cellphone service, and no staff meetings. Just the sound of the canyon wrens and the wind.* He felt his shoulders ease back into the seat as he contemplated the next few days of rest amidst the solitude.

2

Two Days Earlier

Aeneid Corporation, Anaheim, California

As Dev Leitner stepped out into the warm night air of the parking garage adjacent to the Aeneid Corporation, she saw the glint of a blade as it nearly grazed her right cheek. Another step closer and she would have suffered a grave knife wound to her face. Something primal in her instincts had been aroused a micro-second earlier, causing goosebumps to roll over her neck and alerting her to danger. She had learned long ago never to ignore such signals.

As she dropped her shoulder bag and backpedaled on an angle off to the side of her blue Camry, she caught the image of cold steel coming from a tall man in a blue shirt. Unconsciously, she parried the blow using her right forearm, driving the man's knife hand down and then viciously slamming her fist sideways into his neck muscles. She heard the man gasp for air, giving her an opening to step forward and smash her foot into his groin. He buckled but managed to still flail his blade out at her in a desperate attempt to keep her at bay. The tip of the tactical knife caught her on the underside of her forearm but she hardly noticed the pain from the superficial incision, instead focusing on the man's eyes, which bore the look of a fierce predator and not the crazed meth-head she initially took him for.

She glanced down at her shoulder bag. In any other case she would have bolted and left the perpetrator to her belongings but this was too valuable. Her entire life was inside there, though it seemed it was also now in her own hands.

Dev knew it was unlikely anyone in the area would come to her aid as it was ten o'clock at night and she had already seen to the security cameras in the garage being disabled.

She could see the exposed butt of a Beretta pistol bulging out from the thin man's beltline. Dev's thoughts quickly returned to the offensive and her years of Krav Maga training sprang to the forefront as the attacker rushed forward in a partial stagger, slashing wildly, his formerly refined movements diminished from his injuries.

She angled off to his right, blocking the knife hand again with another parry while smashing her heel down across the top of his instep. The attacker crumpled, going down on one leg while she drove her elbow into his face, sending him to the asphalt. She retrieved the blade from the ground beside him and kneeled by his head, the tip of the edged weapon pressing against his carotid while she removed the pistol from his waist.

As the man lay groaning, he muttered in between breaths, "We found the software mole you installed. Did you really think you could steal data from the mainframe without getting caught? You're done for."

"It's your boss who's finished," she said while inspecting the tiny surface wound on her forearm.

Dev stood up, moving out of reach of the man while she pulled the slide of the Beretta back to perform a partial chamber check and scan for a round inside. She glanced around for any other assailants while flipping the safety of the pistol off and pointing the weapon at the grumbling figure on the pavement.

Dev looked down at the man, studying his chiseled face which resembled that of a groomed professional soldier like she had grown accustomed to seeing at her workplace. Aeneid was one of the largest defense contractors in the U.S. and provided their small army of trained mercenaries to third-world governments around the globe though few in the public knew that. For seven months, she had labored undercover at Aeneid to gather the critical intel on the nefarious business undertakings of the company's CEO, Nelson Ritter. *The thought of spending another second in this den of insanity is going to cause me to retch. This assignment was way more than I bargained for. I need to get the hell out of here.*

She glanced down at her leather shoulder bag and then resumed her attention at the sound of an approaching vehicle, its tires screeching in the street below. "Shit, they're onto me this fast," she yelled, rushing to grab her bag while keeping the pistol trained upon the injured man, whose mouth was gurgling out blood with each word.

"You can't get away from him. His eyes are everywhere. You know that," he said in a bronchial voice. His face became ashen as he struggled to suck in a breath and finally went unconscious.

Dev could hear the vehicle closing as it rounded the last

bend in the avenue below the parking structure. She leaned over the man and combed through his pockets, removing a flip phone and a billfold with fifty-dollar bills secured in a gold clip. She stood up and scanned the exit doors.

Dev ran along the pavement, bolting down the stairwell two steps at a time. She flipped the Beretta safety back on and tucked it into her appendix region under her jeans. Coming around the corner, she saw another security officer headed towards her, thirty feet away. She spun to the right but ran directly into the chest of another guard, a bearded goon who grabbed her by the hair. "Not so fast, bitch."

She drove her index finger into his eye, causing him to reel back, then she swiftly delivered a low kick to his knee, hearing the side of the patella crack. The man fell forward and she deftly removed his pistol. All of the years of repetitive drills had saved her life and she was grateful for the hard-earned skills her father had imparted to her growing up. She turned to face the other guard, who had come to a halt eight feet before her. They met with their weapons extended at each other's faces.

"You didn't disable all the cameras. We have you stealing corporate files." He looked down briefly at the disabled guard, who was bawling. "And now two counts of assault."

"Better make that three," she said, firing a round into his shoulder then peeling off to the left between two cars. The two guards' constant shrieking echoed off the concrete walls as she slunk away. She stood in the shadows near the ground-level garage entrance and peered ahead through the door as a white security van sped up the parking structure ramp.

Dev waited until they were out of sight and then sprinted across the street towards a bar. She made her way to the restrooms and then made an abrupt turn for the rear exit door at the last second. She crept along the vacant alley and slid down into a cement aqueduct behind the storefronts, trotting for a half-mile along the trash-strewn corridor until she arrived at an intersection below the highway. She paused and pulled out her work phone. Dev removed the sim card and smashed it on a rock with her boot heel. She activated the guard's phone and scanned the last few numbers. All of them indicated they were restricted except one whose numbers showed in blue. The area code indicated Phoenix, Arizona. She committed this one to memory, reciting the digits several times, then flung the device on the ground.

Her mind raced and her pulse quickened more so now than it had during the fight. She felt trapped, like there were crosshairs upon her. She clutched the shoulder bag close to her and inspected the critical contents: the palm-sized micro device she had used to force pairing with Aeneid's mainframe, the flash drive containing the data that implicated Aeneid, and her forged identification documents were all present. Everything for which she had put her life on the line for so long was safely in her possession. Her work at Aeneid had provided the proof she needed about the CEO's involvement in multinational corporate espionage and a lone-wolf terrorist attack that somehow involved the Iranians. Now she just had to uncover the timeline and hopefully unravel this plot before it was unleashed.

She quickly ran through her list of options, knowing she would be on the run, never able to return to her apartment or former façade of a life. For the past seven months she had gone by the name Mira Sanchez. Her dark Israeli complexion, multi-lingual skills, and raven hair allowed her to blend into a variety of ethnic backgrounds. With her forged documents and passport, she could slip by the eyes of the TSA and most database systems. Her undercover assignment working in cyber security at Aeneid was connected with an operation two years in the making and it had consumed her life. She'd had no time for visiting the coast, sightseeing, or any of the other pleasantries Americans enjoy when they come to L.A. The data files she had acquired were all that was holding her here now.

Dev reached in her pocket and retrieved a small encrypted cellphone. She'd carried it for months but this was the first time she had need of it. She tapped on the only preloaded number on the menu. A few seconds later the raspy voice of an older man answered, his Israeli accent barely noticeable.

"I've been compromised here," she said. "I have the data. They're planning a series of lone-wolf attacks with sleepers around the Southwest but I don't know when. There is a link to Phoenix that I need to track down. There isn't time to wait for you and your team to assemble in the U.S. I need to move on this now."

There was a pause and then the man spoke. "I have someone in that city—an old associate that can be trusted. I will text you his location. Once you get there, lay low and make contact with me in 48 hours."

"Roger that." As she went to hang up, she heard the man's voice soften in tone. "And stay safe—remember what I've taught you, Devorah."

She shoved the phone back in her pocket, listening to the maddening swish of traffic above her and relishing the comforting aroma of cedar trees which reminded her of home in Tel Aviv. She inhaled deeply, embracing the fragrance. *Time for a change of scenery—the desert beckons, it seems. My mission is almost over—I hope—I pray. Then I can return to my country and my parents once more.*

3

PHOENIX, **Present Day**

MITCH DROVE his dusty green jeep up I-10 then hopped onto the less congested Highway 101 which carried him across the east valley. Though it was Sunday, drivers were still bent on exceeding the speed limit by fifteen miles, tailgating and zipping between lanes without signaling. For a moment, he was glad that he was not on the metro Phoenix Police Department or he'd have gotten in his daily quota of speeding tickets within the hour.

He stopped at the Safeway grocery store in Cave Creek on the edge of the desert. He loaded up on a twelve-pack of cold Corona beer along with enough trimmings for making enchiladas for dinner.

Driving along the sinewy dirt road that led out of the small town, he skirted along Cottonwood Creek for eighteen miles until he arrived at the ranch entrance which was little more than a wrought-iron gate beside a stock pond laced with cattails. As he stepped out to unlatch the lock, he noticed a set of boot prints in the dusty soil of the road which overlaid the older tire tracks of the ranchers leading out from last night. The pattern had two oval figures in the heel section and lightning bolt-shaped lines running up the center towards the toes. There was a slight micro-tear, a mere crack, on the right shoe near where the little toe would be. The shoe size indicated a size seven or eight and the slender contours of the inner arch revealed it was most likely a woman though there were no absolutes in tracking. You gathered all the data you could from the ground and your surroundings and made your best guesstimate. This time, though, he was puzzled by the unfamiliar tread and hoped his precious days off wouldn't be consumed with a search.

Mitch figured the tracks probably belonged to one of the owner's daughters who may have stayed behind. The only other person at the ranch was Miguel, an old, nearly deaf Mexican cowboy who rarely ventured off his front porch anymore. Upon careful scrutiny of the tracks on the road ahead, he could see that the person had a short stride which meant she was either carrying a heavy load or was tired.

Mitch backtracked and saw the prints coming in from the right side of the road, opposite his approach. He walked a hundred yards up until he came to a bend in the road and noticed that there was a green Nissan parked under the shade of a sycamore tree. The vehicle was angled back behind a fallen branch and it appeared to be a rental with only a crumpled map on the passenger's seat and some empty water bottles on the floor. *Hmm...probably another dumb tourist who broke down looking for lost Apache gold.*

He retraced his steps and unlatched the gate, swinging it open on its creaky hinges. He drove down the narrow road past the main houses, waving to old Miguel who was sitting on a rocking chair on his porch. The man did a partial attempt at a wave and Mitch could tell he had woken him. Heading down the road, he saw the usual slew of black cows grazing in the field to the left, near the edge of the rim where his bunkhouse was situated.

Mitch kept hoping that he wouldn't have to render assistance to some dehydrated explorer waiting on his porch steps. Cellphone coverage was spotty, especially in the basin where the ranch was nestled, and he dreaded having to drive someone out even for a few miles to get reception. He just wanted to unwind in the shade without anyone demanding his time. All the same, he kept his seatbelt off so he could access the Glock on his hip just in case it was more than a stranded motorist.

Arriving at the front of the historic adobe structure with its white-flecked paint clinging tenaciously to the clay foundation, he got out of the jeep and observed the ground. The tracks had meandered around the other structures on the property and stuck to the treeline near the rim until arriving at his place. Given the hard substrate of gravel, most of the tracks were faint but he had pursued insurgents over much more challenging terrain in other regions and could pick out the subtle disturbances.

Unusual for the average person to cling to cover like that. Based upon the 'dwell-time' where there is greater track depth and tread detail present when a person stands in one place versus walking, he figured the person spent a few minutes near the corner of each building, scanning the field ahead. This wasn't feeling like a lost hiker as he'd encountered before at the ranch.

He moved back to his jeep and retrieved his M4 out of the rear locker. Through experience in government-sponsored missions abroad in the military, he had learned that when the tracks don't provide enough information, you have to rely on intuition. Trackers the world over recognized that your subconscious collects far more data from your surroundings than your conscious mind. His gut was telling him something was off and it was further confirmed when he saw the tracks skirt around his bunkhouse and head up a slope towards the water tower behind his dwelling.

He was without any kind of field support from his colleagues or the sheriff's department. Even if he could get a call out, it'd be over an hour before they arrived. Maybe it was some thief hoping to break in and steal some of the vintage cowboy accoutrements lining the walls of the main house or worse yet, some anti-ranching enviro-nutjob who wanted to torch the place in hopes of putting a stop to cattle operations. He'd heard of that happening before on spreads up in Nevada and he sure as hell wasn't going to let it occur to his friend's land. Mitch crept to the edge of the house and peered up towards the water tower forty feet away. It was a bulbous, gray receptacle that stored twelve hundred gallons of water, atop four massive iron uprights. The whole thing resembled a small moon resting upon angled rusty fingers. Directly beneath it was a ten-by-twelve pumphouse whose door was still locked.

Mitch backpedaled to the front of his place and went through the motions of closing and opening the door, loud enough for the sound to carry. Then he stepped off the porch and moved past two large cottonwood trees which had a blue hammock suspended between them. He slid down into a drainage twenty feet below the rim then crept through the thick foliage of raspberry bushes and wild grapevines. Rounding the bend in the wash, he pressed his face between a patch of overhanging leaves and studied the water tower. He had always taught his law-enforcement students that when a fugitive's tracks proceed to high ground then the subject is probably waiting to snipe you from their perch. There had been two game wardens back east who had been killed by poachers using this same technique and Mitch himself had used it on more than one occasion in Afghanistan. *Whoever you are, you picked the wrong ranch to fuck with. I may not even call this one in if you're an anti-ranching whacko.*

He peered through the scope of his rifle and saw a thirty-something woman with dark tussled hair squatting beside the rear of the pumphouse. She had an athletic build with lean arms. Her face bore a tired expression and he could discern a heavy coat of sweat hanging over her forehead. Despite this, she had the poise of someone who seemed comfortable working from concealment. Slung over her back was a leather shoulder bag. Scanning down her left side, he saw she was holding a pistol—a Beretta by the looks of it. Mitch took a deep breath and studied her features again. *She definitely ain't here for the enchiladas. And I sure as hell wouldn't forget a face like that.*

4

INSIDE THE HEADQUARTERS of the Aeneid Corporation, CEO Nelson Ritter was studying a 3-D holographic image of their current operations around the globe with particular attention focused upon Turkmenistan.

Aeneid was recognized as the leader in body armor for police departments, the military, and the executive protection industry. Ritter had once been a soldier of fortune in Latin America during the '80s and later started the company in the U.S. serving the law-enforcement community. He used any profits to slowly start funding his own mercenary operations in third-world countries where his fledgling investments were rooted. Over the ensuing decades his small army of private para-military contractors had been used for implementing little-known coups, staging riots, and swaying political outcomes in countries connected with Ritter's holdings which were mostly in the form of natural gas or oil. Surinam, Guyana, and Eritrea were just a few of the countries where Ritter had oil operations that were kept in play through the use of his private soldiers and the backing of the totalitarian regimes to which he provided considerable compensation. He always opted for establishing his presence in smaller countries with oppressive leaders and away from the prying eyes of meddling human rights groups. These overseas business ventures were kept separate from the rest of Aeneid through shell corporations abroad and few people even within the Department of Defense knew about it thanks to a connection at the upper echelon of the Pentagon.

AT A RECENT DEFENSE contractor's expo in Virginia, Ritter had procured a large contract from international investors that would lead to further expansion of his reach. Corporate stocks had doubled recently after the initial unveiling of a new concealable soft body armor for civilians. Ritter's goal was to use recent terrorist-related events to create a need in the psyche of homeowners and concerned parents that they too should be as protected as the police. The writing easel on the wall used at his daily meetings with his board of directors had numerous reasons highlighted in red ink as to who in America needed Aeneid Armor: postal workers, bank employees, courthouse staff, delivery drivers, single moms with crazed ex-husbands, and even teachers in cities with high violent crime rates. Ritter surmised, with the latter, that if he could convince every gun-toting dad in the country to buy body armor then school districts in Second Amendment-friendly states would also be within reach. His end game wasn't protection—it was just making enough profit to further fund his operations abroad. The same body armor he retailed to U.S. law enforcement was peddled under a different label to Taliban factions and even Somali pirates. Ritter had learned long ago from analyzing his weak-kneed competitors that possessing moral turpitude only served to hamper market expansion.

Ritter had always reveled in his ability to manipulate others. He'd started out working on his father's used car lot after high school and knew the mouth-watering pleasure that came with closing the deal. A year later, broke and bored, he joined the army, doing a stint in Honduras in the early eighties where he fell in love with the tropics and the political climate. After his discharge he stayed on in Latin America, acquiring work with former Columbian military personnel who were running their own mercenary outfits.

Everything was unfolding smoothly with his latest venture until the troubling alert he received two nights ago from building security who informed him of a breach in their computer firewall. A hacker, working from inside, had obtained files from Ritter's own computer on a new paramilitary operation—information that could compromise a potential billion-dollar undertaking and which involved his colleague at the Department of Defense.

As Ritter rubbed his thumb under his lower lip, contemplating the holographic layout in front of him, the wooden double doors opened behind him. Jessica Carter, the company's head of the cyber division, strode in, accompanied by the chief of security Drake Redlyn. The hulking brute was clad in a suit that barely fit his muscular frame and he looked oddly out of place beside the sleekly dressed woman who wore a blue dress with three-inch black high heels. Ritter normally performed his office tasks and Skype meetings from his mansion in northwest Anaheim two days a week and the woman gave a surprised look at seeing her boss.

"Ms. Carter, have you located the whereabouts of our employee Mira Sanchez yet?" Ritter said, walking within bad-breath distance of the two, causing her to take a step back. She saw the hulking figure of Drake, the bodyguard, casually move to her right.

"She was just spotted near Phoenix. Our men on the ground there will have her shortly," said Drake, interrupting.

"Am I to assume that we have containment of this problem?" said Ritter, who ran his fingers through his silver hair.

Carter fidgeted with her fingers. "Yes, the cover story we provided with the feds will be lending a hand to her capture."

"The data file you spoke of is on her?"

"That's not clear yet," said Carter with a nervous exhale.

"Then all of the loose ends are not tied up. I can't have that information floating around God knows where." He walked around the holographic image and gazed at the blue orb. "You do realize this happened on your watch—you hired the woman and trusted her.

"She will be back here shortly so I'm not worried—she was just a mid-level software technician," she said as Drake slowly inched towards her while she cleared her dry throat.

"Mid-level, you say. So her act of penetrating our firewall was a stroke of luck?" He emitted a deep sigh and flicked out a fake smile, the glow from his white-crowned teeth nearly blotting out his lips. "Well, well, if you say she'll be here shortly then my faith in you is restored. Bravo, no harm done." Ritter continued grinning, his lips slowly decreasing in width. He shifted his gaze to Drake, who shuffled forward with surprising grace and swiftly wrenched Carter's head with his bear-like hands, snapping her vertebrae like a fistful of wet twigs. The delicate figure collapsed to the floor like an inanimate puppet.

Ritter moved over to the crumpled woman, shaking his

head. "That is for your lack of foresight in preventing this problem in the first place."

Ritter returned his gaze to the blue image, enhancing a region in Turkmenistan near the Sangar Valley and then tracing his bony finger over to the Caspian Sea. "It's all coming together. We just need this woman back in our clutches. Soon this whole pipeline dispute will be resolved and the killing and drilling can commence. Then oil will flow freely to Europe without the involvement of Iran."

Ritter's thoughts floated back to the next step in his overseas venture. Aeneid was responsible for training a garrison of elite Turkmen troops modeled after Army Special Forces. This required him to send over a team of mercenaries, or as he referred to them, strategic partners, to begin their work training the soldiers. These Turkmen would ultimately be responsible for protecting the pipeline and U.S. corporate interests. The trainers were former spec-ops soldiers hailing from different countries which fell in line with having plausible deniability and avoided appearing like a backdoor U.S operation. If the plan was successful, few in the White House would balk at the end result of weakening Russia and Iran's grip on the region and there would be no need for them to disavow actions that they were completely in the dark about.

If he was somehow connected to the operation, unlikely as that was, Ritter would say he was merely supplying advisors to a fragile geographic neighborhood and was aiding in the war on terror by laying the groundwork for a potential staging area for any future U.S. actions towards Iran. He was assured by his Pentagon connection that such inquiries would never materialize. The Turkmenistan parliament certainly wouldn't disapprove as they were interested in receiving a massive infusion of foreign dollars for providing one of the longest pipelines in the world.

Ritter walked in a circle around the orb, stepping over Carter's body like she was a stuffed animal. "For most of the past fifty years, the American sheeple think the U.S. has been fighting ground wars to protect them when it's always been about protecting American business interests in foreign lands. Corporations not countries determine war and peace. Not that it matters; as long as the masses have their precious Facebook and their Hollywood celebrities telling them what to think, their world will go on."

He turned and walked to the door, stopping at the entrance and glancing at Carter's face. "I'd rather not know the cover story on this one," he said to Drake. "Report back to me with the missing data files in Ms. Sanchez's possession after you've returned from Arizona. I'll be at home going over some operational plans on my computer. We only have a few days until things unfold and we cannot deviate from the timeline." He gave Drake a piercing look. "I need you to find that bitch."

After Ritter left, Drake flung the woman over his immense shoulder like a wet beach towel and carried her to the stairwell six floors down where he placed her on the landing. As he arranged her limbs in a contorted fashion, her lifeless eyes stared upward, resembling the bottoms of two mini whiskey bottles. He removed one of her black high heels and broke off the spiked end, tossing the piece on the stairs above. Then he unscrewed the light bulb in the ceiling and rattled it until the filaments inside broke, twisting it back into place.

In the past six years of working as head of security for Aeneid, Drake had grown fond of the increasing power that Ritter had provided him. He frowned upon the title 'bodyguard,' preferring the term 'problem-solver' instead. Drake slunk off into the darkness, ascending the stairwell to the roof where the company's private helicopter was awaiting his arrival.

Twenty minutes after Carter's demise, the phone of Assistant Secretary of Defense Thomas Monroe rang as he sat at home in his mahogany-lined library in Arlington, Virginia.

He slid his glass of brandy onto the table and grabbed his phone, which was resting next to a pewter-framed photo of his wife and four children.

"Whenever I see your number on my screen, Nelson, it makes me wonder if I'll be getting any sleep."

"There's a slight problem. We had a corporate spy who obtained a file—a file that contains information on our upcoming venture."

Monroe sat erect and his shoulders tensed. "Tell me this is contained."

"It will be. I need you to grant approval for facial recognition software to be employed by one of our agents on the inside so we can pinpoint the culprit's location."

"Listen, you better…"

"Spare me the finger-pointing. If you had provided me with the clearances and funding when I asked months ago, this whole operation would have been underway already so grant the approval with the lackeys on your end and let me do my job."

Monroe took a long pause, trying to calm his nerves. "Very well but keep me informed when you have this under control. I have a budget meeting tomorrow with the sec-def and we don't need any ripples in the media about Iran just yet."

"I wish you a good night's sleep then, Thomas."

Monroe placed the phone down and poured himself another glass of brandy from the bottle beside him, spilling some on the table as he tried to steady his hand. He'd never had reason to doubt Ritter before in all of their business dealings but those seemed small-scale compared to what was at stake this time.

Monroe saw to it that allegations of war profiteering or misappropriation of funds for private contracting never reared their heads in his meetings with the Senate Oversight Committee. His office, which had a $125 million budget, was responsible for overseeing the lucrative defense contracts of which Aeneid held a considerable slice. It was largely through Monroe's efforts that Aeneid went from being a small provider of body armor for law enforcement to a major player in the mercenary trade with millions of dollars in U.S. government sponsored contracts. Prior to his ascension to assistant sec-def, Monroe had been an attorney in international trade in Washington D.C. and on the payroll of many of the defense companies whose budgets he now had the means of manipulating.

This new venture though was unlike anything he'd undertaken before. Since the collapse of the Soviet Union, obtaining oil from the Caspian Sea region had been nearly impossible given the terrain challenges and the divisive politics of the many post-Soviet states. A consortium of American oil companies were interested in ways to obtain a stranglehold on the considerable oil reserves. Ritter was one such puppet-master they sought out through backwater channels. His previous connection with Monroe, through their mutual history of involvement with the DOD, proved beneficial to moving the wheels of geographic dominance forward.

Monroe needed Ritter as much as the old curmudgeon required his services and he was confident that Aeneid's operation would proceed without any bumps—at least until this latest phone call.

He rubbed the back of his neck and then swigged down the rest of his drink, the concern in his eyes slowly melting away with the infusion of liquid courage while he tried to refocus on the forthcoming fiscal tsunami that was about to swell his pockets.

5

Since her arrival in Phoenix, Dev had spent her time tracking the movement of one man within the FBI and was still unsure of who he was. Somehow he was connected with the Aeneid Corporation back in Anaheim. The phone number she found on the dead man's cellphone had given her enough of a trail to use her own surveillance software to locate the Phoenix caller. Now she just had to provide more solid evidence to prove that he was connected with her boss's nefarious undertakings at Aeneid and to prevent the potential attack from occurring. What she didn't know was the big picture—why launch a bunch of lone-wolf attacks around the western United States? What purpose did it serve other than the obvious body count and short-term media frenzy? Something this orchestrated required considerable planning and funding so there had to be more to it than just shock and awe. And what was the timeline—this week or next month?

The coordinates her handler had provided to direct her to a trustworthy former colleague from the spec-ops community had led to this isolated ranch in the Sonoran Desert. Dev wondered how he was connected with her organization back in Israel but had little choice in asking for assistance after being on the run. She had driven by the day before and scouted the location with her binoculars from a distant hilltop. It had appeared that the cowboys were preparing to leave so she decided to wait until the next day and make her entrance then. All she needed was a safe place to lay low for a few more nights and she didn't want to risk staying in Phoenix any longer. She had picked the lock on the first house near the stock pond and obtained some canned goods and replenished her water supply.

As the day wore on, Dev waited in concealment along the thorny treeline for someone to arrive. It wasn't until mid-afternoon that she saw a jeep roll down the road with a lone muscle-head inside. By his swagger and gear, she surmised he was probably law enforcement. Climbing up beside the water tower gave her a better tactical advantage until she could discern for certain if this was her man.

Dev saw the lean figure step out of his jeep and briefly pause to look at the ground. *Shit, I don't think I left any of my tracks down below. They should just blend in with the rest of the cowboys' prints anyway.* She heard the man go inside the house and close the door. Dev kneeled down and peered around the side of the pumphouse to listen for movement, then she crept down the hill towards the back door.

She had never been on a ranch before though she had spent her share of time on desert operations. Those had been in Africa and the Middle East, where she was assisting with her organization's K & R missions. She hated the scarcity of resources for surviving in third-world desert nations and always relished returning home to Israel to enjoy the civilized comforts. The past few days of surviving on the move had worn her out and she felt stiff from inadequate sleep in her vehicle. All she wanted was for this nightmare of undercover work to end so she could resume a relatively normal life apart from the fictional persona that she'd had to endure at Aeneid.

Moving along the wooden porch, she reached for the handle on the door and turned it but then heard a faint sound behind her. Dev spun around and pointed her pistol at a man who had just emerged from the arroyo.

"Drop your weapon," he yelled as he shuffled forward in a smooth gait while aiming his AR at her head. She saw his tactical vest, which indicated he was with the FBI. She kept her pistol grip firm and focused the front sight upon him. Then she let out a sigh and turned her weapon aside, raising both hands. The man kept his attention upon her while darting a quick sideways glance around either corner of the building.

"Easy, I'm not here to cause any trouble. Just looking for someone." The words felt sticky in her mouth as she tried to calm her breathing.

"Yeah, who's that? You don't look like you're here for horseback riding lessons."

"Sergeant Major Mitchell Kearns."

Mitch clenched the grip on his rifle, squinting as he looked her over.

"Who the hell are you? You better start talking fast. I may be with the FBI but I'm also Old West at heart and don't have any qualms about dropping your ass right here and running your prints later."

"My name is Devorah Leitner. I'm the daughter of Anatoly Leitner, who sent me here."

Mitch sucked in a deep breath and tilted his head slightly before lowering his rifle. His eyes widened and he stared at the mysterious woman as a breeze ruffled the dry leaves on the ground behind him.

6

FBI Bureau Chief Evan Ryker was a wiry man with blond brush-cut hair that resembled the bristles on a new toothbrush and belied his investment in hair gel. He was sitting at his desk in the downtown federal headquarters in Phoenix when a high-priority email popped up on his laptop. Clicking it open, he saw two facial shots of a raven-haired woman by the name of Mira Sanchez with the title below indicating: *Upgraded to Ten Most Wanted Fugitive List.*

The bulletin revealed that she was a domestic terrorist and was responsible for a recent security breach at a private contracting firm along with charges of sabotage, violent crime, and weapons violations.

"Subject should be considered armed and extremely dangerous...yada, yada..." Ryker muttered, reading over the last line which he'd seen dozens of times on such warnings each month. He hit the approve button to circulate it to his staff and then printed off copies to post on the main bulletin board in the briefing room. Before getting up to grab the flyers, he picked up the hardline on his desk and called the software analysis technician one floor below.

"This is Ryker. I'm forwarding an email to you about a subject and I want you to run her photo through facial recognition software in and around the city here for any recent hits as soon as approval from D.C. comes in." After he hung up, he stared at the lovely features of Mira. She wasn't the usual pasty-faced criminal with unkempt hair and poor teeth that graced the FBI billboards. "Ooh, too bad such a beauty is so tarnished," he muttered to himself. "Whoever crosses your path is going to be disarmed in more ways than one, I think."

He retrieved the copies from his printer and headed out the door, sliding his reading glasses down on the bridge of his beaky nose, hardly noticing his busy staff as he walked by their desks.

Ryker had been assigned as interim director for the Southwest Division as a stepping stone to a coveted job in Seattle. During the past three months he had slowly come to appreciate the climate and culture of Arizona which contrasted sharply with his former posting at the D.C. office.

With a nice home in the upscale neighborhood of Scottsdale and the pleasant lack of humidity, he was reconsidering his assignment to the dreary Pacific Northwest and thinking about requesting a permanent position in Phoenix.

He walked by his field operators, who were milling around a table discussing an upcoming training event. Ryker nodded at them as he strode over, sliding a copy of the Most Wanted flyer towards them. "Bet you were wishing they all looked like her." He grinned. He patted the man to his right on the shoulder, one of those men whose name he always got mixed up—Dave or Dan—knowing him by his aptitude and qualification scores instead.

When he was finished, he headed downstairs to introduce himself to a group of new recruits fresh from FLETC (federal law enforcement training center). He spent an hour briefing the agents on his expectations, the particulars of the Southwest division, and their work rotations. Near the end of his lecture, he was interrupted by a woman who came down to inform him of the facial recognition trace he had requested. She insisted that the memo was urgent.

He picked up the phone on the wall and spoke with the agent in charge at the D.C. office, a man by the name of Perkins.

"If this is about the woman Sanchez then you should know she's a high-priority fugitive," said Ryker.

"I know. She's been bumped up the list and I'm actually calling to inform you that there's been a hit on her northeast of Phoenix. She was spotted near a gas station in Cave Creek yesterday."

"Very good. We'll get someone on this."

Ryker was pleased things were moving along so quickly. He dismissed the new agents and headed back upstairs. Looked like he would be putting in overtime on a weekend once more. He didn't mind as long as it didn't involve him being outside in the afternoon too much when the temps spiked to triple digits.

7

THE THIRTY-SOMETHING WOMAN'S black hair was pulled back in a tight ponytail, revealing her high cheekbones and olive skin. She had a tiny comma-shaped scar off the left side of her chin. Her almond-colored eyes stared intently at Mitch as if boring a hole through him.

"Anatoly Leitner—now that's a name I've not heard in many years," Mitch said, moving closer to her as she slowly reholstered her pistol while he kept his hands on his rifle.

He thought back to the days when he'd had the pleasure of working with Anatoly Leitner, one of the finest teachers of tradecraft in counter-terrorism that he had ever met. After Anatoly's service with the Mossad, he was hired by several U.S. agencies to provide training to special operations units. The U.S. and Israeli militaries have a long history of sharing training methods and Anatoly was the first of many seasoned combat vets to go freelance after 9/11. After spending nearly a year training Mitch's unit at Fort Lewis and abroad, Anatoly's contract ended and he returned to Israel only to disappear into the shadows again. In addition to being a legendary figure in the world of clandestine ops, he had been like a father figure to Mitch, who had lost his parents at the age of twelve. Now, here was the man's daughter, staring at him with that same look he remembered in Anatoly's eyes—one of controlled fury, like a tempestuous storm at sea about to swallow a ship.

"He mentioned he had a daughter but never spoke much about his family. I only saw a few photos once during a rare barbecue dinner me and a bunch of my old SF buddies had for him before he left."

"So you worked with him in special operations?"

Mitch lowered his rifle, shoving the sling off to the side of his shoulder. "You're asking *me* what your old man did for a living? That sounds like the guy I knew—always keeping everyone in the dark about what he's up to."

He moved a few feet over towards the trunk of a large cottonwood, resting his back against the twisted bark while she stood with her feet shoulder-width apart as if ready to bolt.

"My father never spoke about his work overseas. My mother insisted that when he was home, we would have some semblance of a normal family life that didn't revolve around chaos and warfare."

"So, in other words, no one talked much at mealtimes," Mitch said, giving a knowing look to what she was describing.

She grinned and shook her head. "Yes, it was all a veneer of pleasantries to mask the pain etched in his eyes."

"Anatoly was the best teacher in special operations that I've ever met."

Dev looked him over like a boxer would an opponent in the ring, then she glanced over the trees in the arroyo below. "I need a place to stay for the next few days. There's a potential terrorist attack that is about to unfold somewhere in the southwestern U.S. and I need to piece together all the players."

He thrust his chin forward, chuckling. "Oh, is that all. I thought you were going to say you and your pops needed my help quelling a revolution in Paraguay or some crazy shit."

"Please, can you help me?"

"Did I mention I work for a federal agency? Let me take you downtown and you can present what you know to my bureau chief."

"I can't do that. There's a reason I've been hiding out for the past five days. Someone in the government, in the FBI, is trying to get to me. That's what brought me to Phoenix in the first place. There's a man in your organization who's in on this."

"In on a premeditated attack on U.S. soil—somebody in my agency? Not likely." He moved up to the porch and sat down on a frayed wicker chair beside her.

"Your bureau chief, his name is Ryker, is that right? How well do you know him?"

Mitch raised his eyebrows in surprise at her question. "Not well—he's only been there a few months. Seems typical of government management—lots of Tony Robbins motivational speeches and little action to support it."

Dev remained standing, her body seemingly relaxed on the surface, but Mitch sensed she was on high alert. "I can't say for sure that he's connected but I traced a call to the downtown division that came from my former employer at the Aeneid Corporation in Anaheim after they tried to kill me."

"The defense contractor—the one that makes body armor?"

"That's right. I've been on the inside there for months

trying to track down a connection between them and some intel we picked up from a hostage my father and I rescued."

"Whoa, your father's running his own outfit of spooks? Wait a minute, back up here and pretend I don't know what Anatoly's been into since my days in SF. Your father literally dropped off the radar after he left. He sure as hell never returned any of my calls or emails."

"He's operating his own agency now doing freelance work, mostly involved with liberating hostages—you know, the kidnapping and ransom industry. We run missions all over the world but do a lot of work in Turkmenistan—a place my father is fond of." She shifted her weight to one foot, leaning her shoulder against the wall. "I've been working with him—training, doing field ops and intel. This was my first assignment over here, though, and after this mess I've uncovered, it might be my last for many reasons."

"Now, why would you want to go into that line of work? I mean, don't get me wrong, Anatoly would be the guy to operate under if you're serious about learning the trade but you seem..." He paused, glancing into her eyes and studying the contours of her face. "Well, let's just say that there are other ways to save lives than traipsing around in the shadows of third-world shitholes."

Dev's eyes lit up. "You don't think a woman has a place in..."

Mitch held his hand up, palm facing outward. "Stop right there. That's not what I was saying at all. I've just seen what that work can do to people. How you enter the ranks wanting to do good and help others only to end up needing to mend your own soul years later after dealing with all the horror."

Dev looked out at the canopy of trees where two canyon

wrens were competing for a coffee-colored bark beetle. "You spent a lot of time with my father?"

Mitch shrugged his shoulders. "Around eleven months, nearly 24/7 here in the U.S. or on various overseas operations."

"What I wouldn't have given when I was younger to have such an uninterrupted stretch with him." She ran her hand through her hair while sighing. "But then the wistful prayers of a child sometimes go unanswered, don't they?"

"Let's go inside where it's cooler and you can lay out what you've uncovered." Mitch's trust didn't extend very far with an intruder showing up on his doorstep with a story like she'd just delivered but his instincts told him to hear her out. And no one except a handful of his old SF unit buddies knew about Anatoly so he was pretty certain of her connection, not to mention her subtle resemblance to the man.

"You may not like everything I've got to say. It involves corruption at the highest..." She paused as Mitch raised his hand and then craned his head towards the front of the house.

Something was off. The purple finches that normally nested in the sycamores near the rim were silent and the wind held a musky locker-room scent, the odor Mitch knew was associated with human perspiration. He lowered his body near the edge of the back porch and peered around the side. Moving down the rocky slopes near the main entrance of the ranch were close to fifteen heavily armed men in body armor. The men flowed along the terrain like one organism—a well-trained group who were no strangers to small-unit tactics. They poured over the slope like ravenous fire ants, sweeping their weapons along the upper houses two hundred yards from Mitch's location.

8

"What the fuck is going on?" he whispered, wondering what kind of trouble she had brought down upon his friend's ranch and his own life which only an hour earlier had held the promise of a respite from the chaos of his job.

Dev squatted beside him and gasped as she looked out over the main grounds of the ranch. There were three teams of five men moving in on the upper houses, kicking in the doors and performing sweeps around the structures.

"Aeneid—this has to be Nelson's goons but how the hell did they track me here? I've only used burner phones, moved each night, and..." She paused, biting her lip. "The mole inside the feds must be using facial recognition software. They must have pinged me when I was downtown the other day or in Cave Creek."

"We don't use facial recog on subjects unless they are a high-value target on the top-ten list and even then it takes weeks of red tape and approval with Homeland Security to initiate that."

"Who could circumvent that?"

Mitch smirked. "The bureau chief could but he'd still

need approval from HQ in Washington." He studied the way the men moved, interacted, and their accoutrements, noting their fluid footwork and unison. "These boys seem like heavy hitters—some kind of para-military group by the looks of it."

He clutched his rifle close, remembering Miguel was still asleep on the porch of the uppermost house and realizing that the infirm man was probably unaware of all the commotion. Mitch peered around the side again, looking for a way to reach him when he saw two men ascend the steps to Miguel's house and riddle his chest with gunfire. Mitch's mouth hung open and his throat went dry as he watched the elderly figure slump back into his chair. Mitch slammed his balled fist against the wall. He started to raise his M4 up and then felt Dev's hand on his shoulder.

"You can't engage them. There are too many."

He lowered his rifle, realizing it would be suicidal to attack such a large group. He looked at her with fury in his eyes, wondering what maelstrom she had just rained down upon him.

"Is there another road out of here?" she said, frantically studying her surroundings.

"Nope, one way in, which I used to like until now." He went to the back door and quietly unlocked it, making sure to keep her in his sight. "Help me grab some things from inside then we'll have to make our way out the back along the arroyo."

"Then what?"

"We'll get out of here on foot, but not before I take out as many of those bastards as possible. I'd like our odds better if there were only half as many guys on our trail."

Mitch went into his bedroom and retrieved a backpack jammed with survival gear and spare magazines for his pistol and rifle. On the front flap was a logo that indicated *Zombie Bug-Out Bag*.

Dev scrunched her eyebrows together. "What is it with you Americans and your infatuation with the undead?"

"Just another excuse to buy guns and cool tactical gear, and a man can't have too much of either."

Mitch handed her a scoped Remington 700 rifle and a small daypack with water, first-aid kit, and some MREs. He went into the rear closet and removed some of his reloading equipment, pulling out a canister of gunpowder. Then he ran into the small kitchen at the front and glanced through the tattered white curtains on the window. The men were on their way past the barn and would be headed towards his bunkhouse within minutes.

"Grab a bunch of those beer mugs from the dishrack," he said to her as he pried the lid off the gunpowder. He began pouring the black particles into a half-dozen glasses. When he was done, he reached under the cabinet and pulled out a box of roofing nails and a bottle of bleach. He tossed a handful of nails into each mug while Dev filled a shot glass with the caustic liquid.

Mitch grabbed the mugs and began placing them inside the microwave along with the bleach. She grinned and looked back at him. "I see we've both had the same class in improvised munitions that my father taught."

He looked at her with a mix of surprise and relief, knowing that they might have a chance at getting out of here after all if she was as skilled as she let on and was indeed Anatoly Leitner's progeny. Mitch glanced around the sparse but comfortable surroundings of the old adobe structure, recalling the good times he'd had and regretting the damage he was about to incur upon the historic structure.

She closed the microwave door and set the timer for

sixty seconds. Then they retrieved their gear bags and retreated out the back door. Making their way down into the arroyo, Mitch heard the footfalls of the approaching men as they walked over the parched cottonwood leaves on the ground before the front porch. He glanced down at his watch, counting down the seconds and hoping it would give them the time needed to slip away through the desert.

9

THE FIRST MAN through the door was larger, more muscular than the others. When he entered, four other men flowed in behind him. Maybe it was the mass of the larger mercenary that prevented more from succumbing to the steel shrapnel hurtling through the air when the microwave erupted. Instantly, in a blaze of flame and stabbing spikes, the team of fifteen shooters was reduced by nearly a third. Two more men received a spray of broken glass on the porch as the front windows blew outward, breaking away some of the adobe surrounding the wooden frames.

Drake rushed forward, yelling at his men to retreat to either side and provide support cover as he came up the middle. Standing back ten feet from the front door, which was clinging to the stud by a single hinge, he surveyed the twisted limbs and perforated flesh of the dead men inside. *Fuck me. We don't have a lot of spare guys to draw upon in Arizona. This is going to be a setback if we lose any more assets.*

He scanned the immediate terrain behind the rear of the structure, noting the rock-strewn arroyo below with a backdrop of steep walls on the other side. "She has to be close. That IED was on a timer to coincide with our arrival."

He walked around towards the back, motioning for a few men to follow him. "Search the drainage. There aren't too many places she can go except down there." He yanked another man by his vest and growled at him to help patch up the two injured men by the porch.

When the smoke cleared from the bunkhouse, Drake peered inside then looked back outside at the other buildings. "A bunch of inbred cow-pie lovers," he muttered as he looked around at the rustic dwellings with disdain.

One of his men motioned with a whirl of his hand to a faint trail leading down into the arroyo. Drake nodded for him to continue while he radioed out, knowing he might lose reception once they lost elevation.

"Echo One, do you copy?"

"Bring it," said the man on the other end.

"Four men down, two injured from an explosion. We're on her trail which heads northeast along a drainage."

"Turn on your GPS unit so I can catch up with you."

"Copy that," he said, placing the radio back in his vest, not recognizing the man's voice and wondering who his boss was sending. Drake walked by one of the injured men who was sitting with his back against a tree, wincing and holding gauze over his right cheek. "You ready to move or you gonna sit there and moan like a little bitch?"

The skinny man's one eye widened and his lips parted. He began to stand and Drake extended his gloved hand out to him. "Just kidding. We don't leave our people behind—company policy, you know." He nodded his head at the charred corpses inside the house. "Unless you're dead, of course."

The group moved to the cusp of the arroyo. "Alright,

people, let's roll. She couldn't have gotten too far in all this cactus and rock. It's possible she's with a few others who were here already and they will have a good knowledge of the area so I want eyes up on the ridges for any potential ambushes." He instructed two of his men to return to the main road by the ranch where they'd hidden their jeeps and ordered them to drive north a few miles and await instructions.

Drake led the way down, using the butt of his rifle to push through the thick foliage. He studied the ground, not noticing anything unusual amidst the jumbled rocks. The terrain was impossible to read and he kept mistaking the older disturbances made by horse hooves with the subject he was pursuing, unsure if he was even going the right way. After several hundred yards of slow movement and with his forearms scraped by thorns, he stopped and pulled out a tobacco tin from his cargo pocket, tucking a pinch under his naturally bulbous lower lip. He scanned the arroyo ahead, trying to discern any navigable route through the cactus hell while maintaining an air of confidence with the men on his heels. Occasionally, he'd stop and touch the ground, inspecting some unknown impression and then hoping he was correct in his assumption that it was related to the woman he desperately needed to find.

He knew backup, in the form of a local asset, was on the way but it would be a while before the man arrived. Drake was irritated that Ritter had brought someone else into the picture and hoped it would just be for this brief leg of the operation. *I'm more than capable of taking over the next stage of the mission after we get the woman. I don't need some federal shit-nugget telling me what to do.*

Drake was a rock-solid foot soldier who was excellent at being a blunt instrument, using his considerable brawn to plow through any obstacles that confronted Aeneid or posed a personal threat to Ritter. He'd go to war for the man who had lavished so much attention upon him over the years, even referring to him once during a drunken binge as his wayward son. At least that's what Drake thought he heard. It was enough for him.

10

Two hours later, in the shattered kitchen of the adobe bunkhouse, Ryker and his FBI forensics team were staring at the damage. The wooden window frames were still smoldering while nails and glass shrapnel were embedded in the cabinets amidst mangled corpses spread around the tiled floor. A forest service fire lookout spotter had reported a plume of black smoke emanating from the area that afternoon. After the sheriff's department arrived, they phoned in the information which eventually made it up the chain of command to Ryker as a potential act of domestic terrorism.

He looked over the dead gunmen, removing their masks one by one and studying their faces. Perry had come up on his day off at Ryker's summoning and was trying to piece together Mitch's involvement and possible whereabouts given that he resided at the ranch.

"I got positive ID on two of the perps but the others don't show up in our database," said Perry, who tapped his soiled boots against a bloody corpse whose head looked like it had passed through a wood chipper. "This guy used to head up a security detail in Bogota and the other fellow drove armed convoys through hot zones in Africa. Both were affiliated with some unregistered merc outfit overseas that pulled up in our database."

Ryker put his hands on his hips and shook his head. "What on earth were these guys doing here? Looks like someone's private little army was about to go on a shooting rampage—but why?"

"I spoke with the owners of the ranch. They're up in Prescott. I informed them one of their own had been killed. They confirmed that Mitch was renting out this bunkhouse just as I thought." Perry looked around at the old adobe structure that was partially intact. "Damn, he always said he liked living like a pioneer but I thought he meant going without Wi-Fi."

"Listen, Perry, I know you guys are friends but if there's anything you want to tell me—anything I should know about Mitch's involvement in this..."

Perry rolled his shoulders and smirked. "When I last saw him this morning, he was headed back here. What happened between then and now is beyond me. If he hasn't reported in yet, it's because something went sideways or he's without comms."

Perry walked out the back door and surveyed the ground. He saw a trail through the leaves leading to the arroyo and climbed down past the rock-strewn surface until he was at the bottom. Moving twenty yards to the west, he found a boot print that matched Mitch's tread pattern along with a smaller set that resembled a woman's. To either side were a series of a dozen or more tracks with tread patterns bearing the same design. Mitch and the woman's stride indicated that they were moving quickly while the others were shortened like they were proceeding with uncertainty. Perry took off his FBI ballcap and scratched his head, looking at the challenging countryside then swatting a fly away from his ear. He retraced his steps back to the bunkhouse where Ryker was still analyzing the scene.

Perry glanced at the other buildings strung out around the pasture, amazed that there were no civilian casualties amongst the ranchers. *Would've been a fucking OK Corral shootout if those boys had been at home.*

He squatted down beside Ryker. "They didn't ride a horse or drive out of here. They headed down the wash with a shitload of hostiles in pursuit."

"What do you mean 'they'—I thought it was just Mitch?" said Ryker with a puzzled expression.

"There's a woman's tracks as well. I'd say it's at least Mitch and one other person."

Ryker scratched the back of his neck. "Hmm...interesting. Not sure if there's a connection but there was a sighting of a high-value female fugitive in Cave Creek yesterday—the one on the Most Wanted list that I sent around the office. What are the chances that's a coincidence?"

Perry looked over his shoulder at the parking area and at the homes above where a flurry of field agents were swarming around collecting crime-scene evidence. "Let me take some men with me and we'll get on the trail. Once I get a fix on their location, I'll radio back."

"We can get a helo to sweep the areas around here. No need to get any of our guys tangled up in these canyons."

"Look, I've got fresh sign and a verified direction of travel. You're not going to be able to see that kind of detail from a thousand feet up. Plus, I know Mitch and his methods. It'll hasten our search efforts."

Ryker seemed surprised at Perry's insistent tone but knew he was a skilled mantracker. "If it were anybody else,

I'd say no but take three, and only three men with you and then check back with me at the first sign of Mitch."

Perry summoned the agents, all of whom were new recruits in their late twenties. After the men gathered their assault packs from the vehicle, they headed down into the arroyo. He had worked intermittently with the other agents over the past few months, all fresh out of the academy. Perry took point as he tried to decipher the story on the ground and what had become of his colleague. At the first juncture in the narrow drainage, Perry paused to study the cluster of assorted boot prints in the damp sand while the other men scanned the surroundings, fanning out around him.

Using a South African tracking method, he drew a square with his fingertip on the ground so he had a containment field measuring roughly three feet by three feet. Then he counted each individual heel impression and divided by two, the number that corresponded with the two-legged stride. "Looks like 10 guys passed through here." The method was a reliable predictor for numbers up to a dozen people.

A mile later, Perry looked at the route ahead which wound through cacti and other jagged flora known to impale wayward explorers. He rubbed the back of his neck and shook his head. "This is gonna be some bitchin' terrain to track a bunch of evaders through. Sure hope this isn't a long pursuit."

Ryker came over the two-way radio that was attached to his front breast pocket.

"A helo is inbound and will assist with an aerial search but will have a limited flight window with the monsoon storm brewing to the north of us."

"Copy that; I would concentrate all of their efforts to the northeast."

"I thought you were tracking them to the northwest."

"That's correct but this canyon splits up ahead according to my GPS. I'll cover the area that veers in the other direction. It'll be a better use of our resources."

He clicked off his radio, attaching it to his shoulder sling. "Man, what the hell is Mitch tangled up with?" he grumbled to himself as he began following the contours of the rock-strewn arroyo. "Whatever it is, he's gonna take us on a wild chase through the bowels of hell if I know him."

11

MITCH AND DEV had been trotting along the faint gravel trail for the past mile, snaking their way past boulders that had become dislodged from the rim above as they traveled deeper into the wash which had slowly transitioned into a canyon. Being in such a chokepoint was something he wanted to avoid as it set them up for easy containment and a potential ambush. This was the method the Apaches used to lure U.S. troops during the Geronimo Campaign in the 1880s. The war of counter-insurgency that had taken place in this very region was one which Mitch was intimately familiar with. The Apaches' guerilla tactics were required reading in the special operations community and he found that the exact same methods were of great use across the globe in modern times in Afghanistan, another desert proving ground for unconventional warfare.

As they rounded a curve in the canyon where a large hackberry tree hung out over a huge finger of sandstone, Mitch saw a small spring bubbling out from under the roots. The water trickled over the rocks into the sandy wash and then disappeared in the soil twenty feet away like most desert springs. He stopped in the shade and set down his cumbersome pack, then removed his large fixed blade and began cutting down a handful of finger-thick saplings. He handed several to Dev, who had just swigged down a mouthful of water from the flask in her small pack.

"Sharpen both ends. We're going to use an old Vietnamese mantrap to slow down the goons on our trail." He continued sharpening the tips of the four-foot-long saplings, tossing each one down by his boots upon completion. "Most mantraps you see in the movies are just pure bullshit, done for theatrics. Like the old jungle foot snare that yanks the guy up in the air. Those take around four hours to make and then you gotta have a giant rock on the other end that weighs double your victim to provide the leverage. How the hell is someone supposed to set that up when they're on the run?"

Mitch finished carving the last point and retrieved the newly formed weapons off the ground. "I learned this one from an old marine recon guy who used it on more than one occasion in Vietnam. The natives here also employed this for impaling deer on the trail. It takes mere minutes to set up and can buy you time at the end of the day for getting back to friendly forces."

"What great pals you have. Sounds like some guys I know in my organization—the kind of people you want on your side when the world around you gets ugly."

Mitch craned his head up towards the sylvan canopy of broad-leaved trees. "This world isn't ugly—it's perhaps the only place left that is a temple in the truest sense of that word. It's only man's actions that make things ugly."

Dev stopped whittling for a second while looking at him.

She was surprised by the philosophical tone of someone given to pondering his surroundings in a non-tactical manner. It contrasted sharply with the maiming weapon he was fashioning and she wasn't sure what to make of him. She had worked with plenty of special operations types before, mostly Israeli, and wondered if other American military men were so inclined or if this was peculiar to Mitch.

"So why were you living in that run-down shack back there? You fall on hard times or something?"

Mitch shook his head and emitted a crooked smile. "That 'shack' was my castle in a land of plenty. Far more luxurious than the tiny room I had growing up on my uncle's ranch and anything I stayed in during my army days."

"What did you do for entertainment? I didn't even see a TV," she said with a hint of repulsion.

"There's nothing like waking up to the sounds of the canyon and then spending time working with your hands under open skies. That's the life we were meant to live—not reclining in front of a laptop in a café clicking 'Like' buttons while wondering if the lady at the checkout counter made the foam on your pumpkin-spice latte thick enough."

"Wow—don't sugar-coat things for me, Agent Kearns. I can take it." She chuckled and then resumed preparing the sapling in her hand.

When they had finished carving, making sure the shavings had fallen between the boulders at their feet to cloak their efforts, Mitch walked up the trail. He stopped at a point where it meandered between heavy clumps of overhanging tree branches then he drove the half-dozen spears into the ground on a sixty-degree angle so one end protruded towards the incoming trail. "This heavy foliage will obscure the traps, causing the lead guy to get impaled where it counts," he said, pointing to the groin area. "Such traps are designed to maim and slow the pursuers down and will sometimes even cause them to reconsider whether they should continue the chase."

"You ever have to use this before?"

"Not here, but I've seen dope fields in the mountains outside of Phoenix with this setup. It'll make you think twice about where you're hiking."

He grabbed his pack and picked up some handfuls of water, splashing it over the tracks they'd made to make it look like they were filling up on water. Once he'd manicured the area enough, they carefully skirted around the mantraps and continued heading north through the serpentine canyon until they found a horse packer's trail leading up. A mile further, they veered off to the right in a side canyon, making a few obvious tracks in the sand. After a hundred yards, they backtracked, making sure to step on rocks to conceal their movement.

"Dummy trails like this don't take a lot of time to make but can buy you some time at the end of the day in getting away," Mitch said. "We'll head up the other canyon and hope they get hung up in this one for a while."

They resumed their travel along the larger canyon to the northwest, picking up their pace while skirting around the clusters of prickly pear cactus and agave. As they crested the shrub-choked rim, Mitch squatted low to avoid silhouetting himself. Ahead of them were miles of open mesa interspersed with occasional juniper trees which stood out like lone sentinels and provided the only shade in the otherwise bleak landscape. Four miles distant was a ridgeline in the limestone which revealed rows of caves, their darkened cavities resembling sunken eye sockets.

"We've got just over an hour of daylight left," Dev said, glancing at her watch. He nodded in confirmation, looking at the position of the sun on the horizon which was nestled below a massive blood-orange thundercloud.

"Caves—God I hate being in caves. I spent half my time in Trashcanistan scouring through caves or hiding out in them," he said, scratching the stubble on his chin. "Let's head there for now. It'll give us a good tactical overview of the area and we can rest for a bit."

"I don't need to rest—do you?"

His forehead wrinkled and he cast an irritated glance at her. "Of course not but with us pushing so hard I don't need either of us wrenching an ankle—that'd put a damper on our retreat real fast, don't you think?"

"I think you are always used to being in charge. I don't mind that in this situation but you can talk with me instead of issuing commands, that'd be a big help."

"You mean the fucking situation you brought down upon me when you showed up on my doorstep? The one that ended the life of a dear old friend of mine?"

She lowered her head, brushing a strand of black hair off her face. "Look, I'm sorry. I didn't mean for this to…"

He stood up and started walking, cutting her off. "Let's go, I'll sort this out later."

For the past hour since their hasty departure from the ranch, he'd only had time to think about their escape. Now, the gravity of the situation struck him in the gut like a boxer's right hook and he felt waves of fury rush over him. He had always been on the right side of the mission and the law. Now he wasn't sure what he was up against and what this woman's end game was. They needed to keep pushing on. Hopefully, there'd be time later for learning more about the details of the operation she had uncovered but first they had to put some distance between themselves and their pursuers. He forced his feet forward, plowing through the ankle-high scrub, keeping the distant caves in his focus like a boat captain navigating through murky waters amidst a jagged shoreline.

12

Perry discerned Mitch's desert boots from the jumble of others as he wove his way through the tangled wash of briars and boulders. The faint impression showed the Danner brand boot tread which Mitch always wore and that Perry knew well. Mitch was evidently moving fast given the displacement of the track in the soil and the kicked-up edges. The actual term was 'dishing,' which happened when the toe portion kicked back a dish of soil onto the midsection of the print. Perry recognized that dishing meant that the subject was either trotting, sprinting, or carrying a heavy load. A shorter stride would be indicative of the latter while an increase in stride with dishing meant the subject was running.

In this case, Mitch inadvertently left a slight toe print in the wet soil near the spring which could mean he was either in a hurry or tired and getting sloppy. Perry knew Mitch had the endurance of a mountain goat and that this rare sight in the soil was due to the fact that he was being pursued. What Perry didn't understand was how Mitch was involved.

He pulled out his GPS unit to check the coordinates and

then looked up at the canyon walls to match the features that were showing on his screen.

Perry and his three men rounded the bend in the arroyo where he saw faint movement fifty yards ahead. A group of men dressed in para-military gear were walking single file, their heads scanning the rim ahead. He raised his hand in a fist, motioning for his team to stop. He waved his hands to the right and left, indicating he wanted them to fan out around him while he went up the middle. Perry saw the group ahead disappear into the foliage. A large man who was at the rear issuing orders to the others turned and then slunk off into the undergrowth.

As Perry moved forward, the muffled sound of a single bullet sliced through the stout operator's neck to his right, spraying a v-shaped pattern of red mist over the sandstone slab behind him. Another round tore through the lower jaw of the tall man on Perry's left while the third man was struck in the forehead. His bone fragments showered over the manzanita bushes, sending a flurry of now-crimson butterflies skyward.

Perry raised his weapon and steadied his gait, his attention focused ahead. The large man from the grove emerged with six others behind him and began moving towards Perry, their weapons fixed on the terrain on either side.

"Only three—I thought you'd have a whole fucking platoon with you," said Drake. He squinted at Perry and glanced over the man. "Good thing you sent me a photo of yourself on my phone earlier. You fucking feds all dress the same."

Perry lowered his rifle, his gaze centered on Drake. "Just glad these were the newbies in the unit. It'll be easier to explain their deaths," said Perry. "How far away are the two fugitives?" Perry reluctantly spit out the last word, still puzzled as to how Mitch was involved in this.

"Two? I thought it was just the woman?" said Drake.

Perry rolled his eyes and pointed to the damp sand, presenting his evidence. "Surprised you made it this far. They've probably gotten a good lead on you by now."

"We've been fifteen minutes behind them since we left the ranch but that gap keeps growing as this fucker's a ghost."

"We're on his turf. He's FBI as well as a seasoned combat tracker." Perry heard some of Drake's men grumble at his statement and cast concerned glances at each other.

"He's going to be pushing forward with a few sideways dummy trails every mile or so to throw us off. He knows he has to get out of the region as quickly as possible before the search envelope folds in on him." Perry looked at his GPS unit again, pulling up the topographic map for the area. "My guess is that he will head northwest until he can get up on the mesa and then make a beeline for the highway."

While Drake's men removed spare magazines from the dead agents, Perry got on the radio to Ryker, simulating transmission interference by issuing a garbled message. "This is Alpha....Team...over."

"Go ahead."

"In pursuit...hostiles, heading....east. No sign of....primary subjects."

When he was done letting the static linger for a few seconds, Perry turned off his radio then moved back towards Drake.

"Ritter said that you were in need of my mantracking skills so I'll take point on this leg of the operation."

"He told me you were at my disposal as an advisor. I'll let you know if I need any help, pal."

Perry looked at the hulking figure's forearms, which had numerous small lacerations from bushwhacking, then glanced down at the man's nearly brand new, fresh from the box boots. "Back at Aeneid, you must be the top dog, but out here things are different. One of your guys steps on a Gila monster or runs into a javelina, it'll only slow us down and allow our subjects to slip away." Perry's eyes remained unflinching as he took a step closer to Drake. "I'm guessing the old man told you to wrap this up quickly without a lot of attention being drawn to your presence here, am I right?"

Drake nodded, taking a step back. "Alright, lead on then, but you run anything by me first when it comes to major decisions."

A few minutes later, a short man with a thick goatee came over, holding a blood-soaked wad of gauze in his hand. "Jameson is not looking good."

Perry gave the man a puzzled expression until Drake spoke up. "He walked into a bunch of punji-type sticks on the trail."

Perry shook his head in disgust as he walked with Drake to the swath of hackberry trees where a man was lying on his back in the shade. He saw the remains of the mantrap and looked at the moaning figure whose upper thighs were perforated with several jagged holes. "Ah, Mitch—you always did like the old-school shit."

Perry shuffled forward towards the injured man, who appeared to be in his late twenties with powder-blue eyes. "That's a nasty wound, son. Let me help you with that." In a fluid motion, he flipped open the folding knife from his pocket and slashed the man's throat. As the desperate figure clutched his gushing carotids, Perry stood up and looked at the other mercenaries who'd gathered in a circle, looking on in shock.

Perry stabbed his blade into the sand, removing the blood, then stood up. "Everybody clear on how I work? You fuck up out here, some coyote is gonna be shittin' out your remains tomorrow."

The men's faces grew solemn and they focused their eyes squarely on Perry, averting their gaze as he glanced at each one of them. He rested his eyes on Drake, who had a startled demeanor cloaked by a veneer of anger. The brutish figure exhaled deeply and then looked away.

Perry unslung his rifle and walked through the center of the group back to the trail. "Good, now let's push on and wrap this up by sundown."

13

Mitch and Dev sprinted from tree to tree, covering a hundred yards at a time. This gapping burst allowed them to cover sufficient ground quickly and protected them from the injuries associated with running long-distance over rocky terrain with cumbersome packs.

Having studied penitentiary escapes, he found that most convicts face-planted in the first two hundred yards and sustained a fractured tibia or sprained ankle, thus ending their flight. He trained guys in his own Special Forces unit to do an initial hundred-yard dash to cover, take a breath and then assess the route ahead before continuing. Tossing in a few sprints in the opposite direction from your dominant step would also contribute to eluding pursuers as eighty-five percent of people are right-handed and will eventually arc in that direction when walking long-distance.

After several rounds of bolting to cover and analyzing the landscape, they arrived at the edge of the mesa. They had to drop down into a shallow canyon and then skirt up to the caves on the opposite side. There were close to forty caves peppering the ridge across from them. Mitch looked for the ones that had paths leading to the mesa above, which would provide an escape route out.

"Why are we stopping, Agent Kearns?" said Dev, who wasn't showing any signs of being winded.

"It's Mitch. I'm just searching for the best way, unless you know a better route."

She exhaled deeply and put her hands on her hips. "I just want to get out of here and back to a city so I can finish what I started. I need a fucking laptop in my hands, not a map."

He motioned to her to follow him down off the ridge along a faint deer trail. "Back at the ranch you said you had the files that implicated Aeneid?"

"That won't be enough. I need to open the file and get further information on the attack. I didn't have time to do that when I was there making the copy other than seeing a few pertinent details. Without that all I have are two guys emailing about some nebulous undertaking in the Caspian Sea region."

"This guy Ritter, what's his story? How did he come to be such a major player in this proposed attack?"

She clenched her jaw, taking a deep breath. "That son of a bitch is a master raconteur like no other. He could talk a bushman into buying hand warmers. The man had some inkling of military service in Central America back in the day. He and some of his soldier of fortune buddies pooled their resources and connections to start Aeneid, leveraging their contacts in the defense industry. Eventually, Ritter bought out all of his investors over the years until he retained full ownership. His off-the-books mercenary agency provides private soldiers for hire to regimes all over the globe."

"That's nothing new. The world of ex-military contractors is a huge industry. Hell, I've had offers myself over the years to run security details for dignitaries in other countries. The money was enticing, like $750 a day plus my own vehicle and house."

"So what stopped you?"

"Mmm...the work was too sketchy. I've had friends that picked up those gigs and were rock-solid guys but they were asked to cross the line on occasion, if you know what I mean, and that's not a place I wanted to go."

"Yeah, well, Ritter has plenty of people at his disposal who don't share your outlook. Only now he and his cronies want to expand their empire to the Caspian Sea."

Mitch tilted his head up, sniffing the air. "Smells like we're near a cow watering hole."

"Is that why you're always sniffing the air like a dog?"

"I wish I had my dog with me. He'd be a good sense multiplier, not to mention being great company." Mitch glanced at Dev, noticing her irritated glance. "Not that you ain't a blast. I mean, shit, this is just what I wanted to do with my time off."

"I didn't see your dog back at the ranch."

"Nah, he's, uh...he's with my ex-wife. She thought it best to hang on to him with my being gone so much."

She shook her head and smirked, making a weak attempt at trying to lighten the mood with humor.

"What, you don't think I'd be a good dog owner?"

"No, just trying to imagine someone being married to you."

His expression grew serious. "I got the right mind to leave your city-girl ass out here. You sought out my help, remember—not the other way around. I was supposed to be enjoying some down time. Before you came along, my life was just fine...just fine."

He pushed past her, leading on through a winding route over slickrock to conceal their tracks then dropping down into a shallow basin that looked like a meteor had slammed into it thousands of years ago. As they trekked during the remaining light of dusk, they stayed silent, both of them embroiled in their thoughts and what the night would bring.

14

With only a hint of light left in the west, they followed the narrow ledge that skirted along the second row of limestone caves until they reached the third level. Mitch scanned the dim entrance ahead to make sure there were no rattlesnake surprises and then crouched and walked inside. While the back recesses were dark, he could tell from the auditory clues and passage of the wind that it only went back a short distance. He squatted along one side of the entrance while Dev kneeled beside the other.

"Where are we?" she said, casting her eyes wide upon the eerie blue-gray landscape below for any signs of movement.

"Henderson Flats region, I believe. This area of the Sonoran Desert has ridge after ridge of honeycombed caves like this. We should be safe here for a while."

He cleared his throat and glanced over at her face in the faint light. "You started telling me some things back at the ranch and on our little nature hike. You wanna finish that conversation and fill me in on what the fuck is going on?"

She finished the last of her water and sat silently as if she hadn't heard his request.

He turned and gave her a penetrating look. "I'd like some answers on how your father is involved in this and your background. By the way you handle yourself and what you've described doing at Aeneid, I'd say that came from more than weekend outings twice a year with your old man."

"I was just a rank-and-file soldier who did four years of military service and then got into the cyber security field afterwards with several different civilian corporations."

Mitch looked over at her, motioning with his hands to continue. "And..."

She stared at the rising moon and then leaned back against the smooth limestone cave, finally relaxing her shoulders. "When my father returned from training what must have been your unit here in the States, he and some of his old colleagues from the Mossad started their own agency." She rolled her boot over a twig on the ground, snapping it in half. "My mother was furious that I developed an interest in his tradecraft. It put a real strain on our relationship as she always wanted me to get a regular job in the civilian world that didn't involve guns or fighting."

She rubbed her hand along the back of her neck. "My father put me, like any new recruit, through the same rigorous training that he had endured in Mossad—all except the assassination part, for which I am grateful. I am not cut out for that kind of work—killing someone in cold blood. However, I was good at the undercover aspect and negotiating with captors along with knowing a few things about computers."

"Yeah, well, it looks like his training paid off. You're still alive." He paused and then sat down across from her.

"My father's company employs former Mossad, SAS, and other ex-special ops personnel. In addition to field operations, we also have our own cyber security division and a proprietary malware that can force pairing with another computer to read its information. That's how I was able to get past Aeneid's firewall."

"What led you to suspect Aeneid in the first place?"

Dev folded her arms across her chest. "We rescued a subject in Turkmenistan who had been captured by rebels that had attacked an oil rig in the Caspian Sea. He was connected with a group of American businessmen sent there to broker a deal on a gas pipeline that would run from the Caspian Sea to Europe, effectively cutting Iran out of the supply. His family had contacted us after he was abducted and all the usual diplomatic channels were exhausted."

She ran her shirt sleeve over her forehead wiping away a sweat-riddled layer of grit while she continued. "The mission went as planned. We successfully freed the captive but he was a destroyed man; his captors had peeled his psyche back too far. He began spilling out details about a deal involving Assistant Secretary of Defense Thomas Monroe and Aeneid's ties to the Caspian Sea pipeline. We were on our way back to the United States the next day with him, thinking his memory would become more lucid once he had time to recuperate and get therapy. Only someone intercepted him after the hand-off to your state department."

Mitch's mouth was agape. "Thomas Monroe from the Pentagon is knee-deep in this shit-show?"

"It would seem so. All we had was this hostage's loosely woven tale but once we began looking into Nelson Ritter, it was clear his company had provided mercenaries to various dictatorships in Turkmenistan, Azerbaijan, and Kazakhstan. That's where I came in, going undercover at Aeneid."

She clasped her knees to her chest while letting out a sigh. "The data file I intercepted implicated a group of Iranians in the U.S. who were going to launch a series of lone-wolf attacks using weapons obtained from Aeneid. Weapons that are slated to arrive in the next forty-eight hours. But where? And when is the attack supposed to occur —those are the things that have kept me awake these past few nights."

Mitch scooped up some sand and let it filter between his calloused fingers then tossed the rest against the rock wall as his face turned grim. He thought about how his world had just made an abrupt turn, like a vehicle that had spun out on an icy bridge and tumbled into frigid waters. He'd had enough of covert operations when he was in the Special Forces and had worked hard to set up his life in a job that allowed him to use his specialized skills but that provided more clarity of purpose and accountability.

Now, he was on the run and there was a traitor in his own FBI field office—but who? The effects of the heat and the day's events were causing his head to throb. All he was certain of was that his career and reputation had the potential to be swept away in the fierce current that washed up at his door with Dev's arrival. It was like his old life was sucking him back in and Anatoly was the fisherman at the reel. He needed to get out of the wilderness and get some answers. If he could locate the mole then he could possibly work from the inside to help thwart Aeneid's plans if there was time. Though, Mitch mused, if the assistant sec-def was involved in this fantastical story then who else was on his payroll?

Dev took in a deep breath and then another, her head swiveling to their right. "Is that cedar?"

"Close—it's juniper. The two trees look and smell a lot alike but we don't have any true cedars in Arizona," Mitch said laconically, pointing to a cluster of junipers on the slopes beside them as his head still swam with the details of Dev's story.

"When my father was on leave at home, he and I would always spend the evening after dinner sitting in the small grove of cedar trees in our backyard. That fragrance is always so comforting to me."

Dev picked up a broken twig and snapped it in half, smelling the bark. She tucked it in her shirt pocket and then looked over at him. "So where do we go from here?"

"We need to make our way overland towards the interstate. From there, we'll hopefully have cell reception and we can use your phone to call my bureau chief and fill him in on the intel you've uncovered."

"Assuming he's not on Aeneid's payroll," said Dev.

Mitch hissed out a breath. "Ryker, ah, shit—maybe. He's a pretty unimpressive guy—like a houseplant that talks. Crimony, who knows if he is—this whole thing is fucked up."

Mitch did a scan of the distant horizon and then shook his head. "Unfortunately for us, we're in a region where there are few cell towers, though I never used to mind that until now."

He arched back, staring out beyond the lip of the cave at the sky. "It looks like those dark monsoon clouds to the north are going to be dumping on us soon. Normally, we'd want to stay put in such weather but that rain will provide good concealment for our passage and obscure our tracks along the mesa above."

She sighed and looked at him. "I'm afraid we're Velcroed to each other until we can find a way out of this region."

Mitch glanced up, studying the contours of the moon that stood like a cloaked orb over the silent valley below. Being cut off from the outside world made him feel like he could be back in Afghanistan on a long-range mission that no one knew about. There wouldn't be any combat search-and-rescue choppers flying over the horizon. They were completely cut off with a team of ruthless mercenaries on their trail. Interstate 17 was still another twenty miles away with some of the most treacherous terrain in Arizona between them and their destination.

If they were to make it there by sunrise, they'd have to push the limits of endurance in a brutal landscape. He was sure his pursuers would be equipped with night-vision or infra-red devices and potentially even drones. Would it be enough to overcome the technology working against them on the other end? He wasn't sure any longer and his mind reflected back on the guerrilla tactics used by the Apaches in this same region over a century ago, when manpower ruled and modern technology was non-existent.

As if sensing his thoughts, Dev stood up beside him. "Even if we dispatch the teams pursuing us, we can't remove the greater threat orbiting the sky miles above our heads which can track our every move with satellites. They'll just keep sending in more teams to this location. I'm probably preaching to the choir but time and distance are our greatest allies. We need to get out from under the radar as fast as possible."

He clenched his fists and took a deep breath then grabbed his rifle. He could hear the strength of Anatoly flowing through her words and wondered for a minute if he was in the presence of his old mentor.

"Let me work my voodoo out here and give these guys a chase they won't live to talk about. After that, you can guide us through the keyboard wilderness."

The soil had changed from the fine sugar sand they had been hiking in the arroyo to a clay-limestone base with a fine surface of talcum-like dust. Mitch was intimately aware of the nuances of each surface and what the likelihood was of having tracks retained in the different soils. Some, like the type they were on now, would blow away with the first gust of wind, eroding any tread details but retaining the foot outline in the compressed impression beneath. The key to counter-tracking was all in route selection: choose a path that had plenty of rocks, logs, or hard surfaces to avoid leaving tracks in the first place.

As he walked, he unconsciously maneuvered around the softer areas, opting for sandstone slabs that would provide concealment of their passage without burning up too much time deviating from their route.

Mitch tore into a pouch of emergency chow from his pack, choking down the dry tablets that tasted like chalk. "Damn, I can see why they're called survival rations." He offered a handful to Dev but she waved them away.

"You need to keep up your energy level."

"Vomiting after eating that won't help."

"Fair enough."

"Besides, I ran in an adventure race last month and did the entire thing on very little food. I will be fine."

Mitch just raised his eyebrows while gagging down the last tablet of chocolate putrescence, then neatly folded the foil packet and tucked it into his vest pocket.

15

Perry was walking point through the canyon, which had narrowed considerably since their last stop. The moonlight wasn't of much help as it was just beyond the cusp of the rim and he had been relying on a specialized purple headlamp for discerning tracks. This color was the best in the spectrum for detecting disturbances on the ground and he'd used it many times on long-distance night searches in the desert, pursuing fugitives with Mitch.

In some ways tracking at night was easier than during the day as you controlled the angle of light. But what you couldn't see was the big picture of terrain features ahead and any potential ambush points. In an agency-wide search, that wasn't usually a problem as you had a hundred guys pounding the ground looking for signs along with horseback and helicopter support. Perry had eschewed the latter, telling Ryker the impending storm would only put more people at risk. He also suspected Mitch would be pushing forward in an all-out march to make it to the interstate and hitch a ride out of the area. At least that's what he kept telling himself he would do if the tables were turned. He knew Mitch was the better tracker and he was glad that he was in a large group that would soon have drone support and vehicles once they could climb out of the canyon.

He passed by a currant bush and then backed up a foot, pushing the low-lying brush aside and directing his light at a wedge-shaped area of sand. Perry knelt down and angled the purple light around the area, noticing a faint heel impression, the half-moon shape barely visible. He walked around the bush, looking for more disturbance, and then swung his headlamp up a faint incline of rocks that led to the rim.

"We head up from here." He motioned to the others with his upright thumb as he resumed leading. He saw Drake staring at the ground with a curious expression.

"You sure this is the way?" said the brutish figure.

"Just as sure as I am about your brain being the size of a walnut. Now shut up and move."

Perry had no desire to huddle around the track and explain to the others what he deduced and how. His heart was racing, knowing that Ritter expected results.

Perry thought about the dead agents a few miles back in the canyon. He felt a tinge of remorse at the skilled men who had met their end. He didn't care that they had wives or kids or were good guys, only that they were fellow warriors who had honed their fighting skills to tremendous standards to be recognized as worthy of being in the FBI. Then he thought about his own skills and his former career aspirations before falling under the spell of Nelson Ritter at a weapons expo in Las Vegas two years previously. Over the ensuing months and through many meetings at the CEO's home, he and Ritter had come to realize they shared the same disenfranchised outlook on working for the federal government.

Perry's own disillusionment went beyond being disgruntled. He was furious at the rejection letters in his personnel file, indicating he wasn't considered a prime candidate for the coveted bureau chief position of the Southwest Division. He figured it was due to his lack of political connections in Washington. He had spent the past decade climbing the regional ladder, attending extraneous social events to further his status, and he had an exemplary performance record. The final straw came nine months earlier when he had been passed over for Evan Ryker, a D.C. desk jockey, who was acting as the new interim director. Perry surmised his goals had tumbled down into an icy crevasse from which there was no return. All he wanted now was the money Ritter had promised then he would depart the U.S. and start over in another country. He thought of opening his own private security firm somewhere that was untapped by Ritter and others like him. There was nothing holding him in America. Even his wife, who was nothing more than a domestic ornament he'd acquired to maintain an image of stability in the eyes of the bureau, was of little use to him now.

Perry figured he would assist with this leg of the operation by capturing Sanchez and then figure out what to do with Mitch when the time came. The sizable funds he was getting from Ritter would help soothe a remorseful conscience, which he hadn't noticed much until a few hours ago.

As the group pushed over the edge of the canyon, arriving on the mesa, Perry flicked off his light. The moon provided enough to see the main terrain features and he suspected that the interstate would be visible in a few miles. The ominous cloud formations to the north were showing signs of lightning discharge and he hoped the storm would hold off long enough for them to get across the open terrain of the mesa.

"Call the men in the jeeps and have them rendezvous with us at the road juncture coming up in two miles," he said to Drake while sifting over the topographic map features on his GPS screen. "From there, you can set up the drones and we can trim off some time locating these two."

When Drake was done relaying the coordinates, he moved beside Perry. "So, this guy that's with Sanchez, he's FBI too—how's that?"

"I keep asking myself the same thing. They obviously have a prior connection."

"This woman has been a fucking headache for Aeneid. She hacks our system, drops a few of our guys, and then disappears only to show up in this rat hole of a state. What's her end game, I wonder?"

Perry just smirked, growing more irritated with each passing minute at the man's presence. "At the end of the day, she probably wants what we all do: peace of mind knowing she made a contribution to humanity and left the world a better place."

Perry's philosophical sarcasm left Drake puzzled, as he'd intended. The disgruntled FBI agent strode onward, hoping the large man would step on a pit viper and give Perry a reason for ending the surly goon whose IQ seemed on par with the boulders around them.

16

The plump moon hung in an obsidian sky, providing enough illumination that Mitch could make out the rock-strewn path leading up the mesa above the caves.

"Next to dodging any encounters with the hostiles on our trail, our biggest concern is going to be inadvertently stepping on a rattlesnake in the rubble ahead," he said as they crept over the rock scree that came off the mesa at a forty-degree angle and was over a hundred yards in length.

Mitch thought back to the time he had been nabbed by a copperhead snake during a sniper training course at Fort Bragg when he crawled too close to a cluster of cattails. That time he was lucky to be in the thirty-percent category of people who receive dry bites each year and he walked away with two vampire-like puncture wounds and a cool story to tell at the bar later.

"Snakes—are they really a problem out here or are you just screwing with me?"

"We're at 3000 feet. The higher elevation means we won't have to contend with as many nasty creepy-crawlies like the lower desert but we still have to be hyper-alert for where we are placing our hands and feet."

"I would have thought scorpions would be a bigger problem out here but thanks for jolting my nerves even more," Dev said as she followed behind him, being sure to step where he had just been. "I remember being in Jordan once and having a scorpion crawl up my field jacket—that was a long night."

"Scorpions—oh, yeah, they're out here too, probably in far greater numbers than the snakes but we're not going to be sleeping on the ground so I'm not as worried. And the cougars on the prowl at night are mainly after mule deer so we should be OK on that end."

"Fantastic—anything else you want to share with me?"

"Well, there was this one time that I stepped on a basking Gila monster on our ranch but..." He paused and turned back to grin, noticing her serious expression. "Just kidding."

"You may be used to crawling around in the brush but I'd rather take my chances in a dark alley in the city than be out here right now. How much farther is the damn highway?"

"Well, it's between not close and too far."

Halfway up, Mitch came across a mangled section of old cattle fencing that had become dislodged from a rock slide. He looked at the tangled heap of barbed wire and then removed the Leatherman from his belt, snipping off a twenty-foot-long section and coiling it up. Mitch made sure they kept their route confined to the rocks so their tracks would be reduced. The Hollywood notion of brushing out your tracks with a handful of twigs did nothing to cover your route but only gave pursuers another type of pattern to search for instead of boot prints.

As they crested the ridge onto the cholla-lined mesa, the landscape ahead flattened out. It looked like one continuous plane that went on for a dozen miles or more with a jagged mountain range as the backstop to the north. Echoing off the rocky walls were the sounds of a pack of coyotes that were working the scrub below for jackrabbits.

Mitch let his eyes adjust to the new visuals while flaring his nose up to take in the odors around them. All he noticed was the constant fragrance of creosote bushes and the flowers of agave whose eight-foot-long stalks jutted up from the earth like desert sentinels. He could make out the faint undulating lights of vehicles on the interstate to the northwest but had underestimated the distance. "Shit, this is going to be more of a trek than I thought."

Dev had come up alongside him and was catching her breath. "As I recall from my military days, the average person can cover around 2-3 miles an hour. That's going to be quite a push."

"That's for the *average* person on level terrain," he said. "In canyon country like this, and traveling at night—*and* if we get dumped on by that storm cell in the distance, I'd say more like 1-2 miles an hour, especially since we're gonna have to stay off the dirt roads."

He looked over at her, noting her athletic figure. "Fortunately for us, we're not the average hikers, are we?"

"Is that your confident side or cocky side shining through?"

He shrugged his shoulders. "Maybe a little of both. Either way, we will make it. Just keep in mind that we're not going to stop every ten minutes to remove cactus spines. We'll patch ourselves up afterwards."

"You're not out with a tourist. I can handle myself out here, perhaps better than you."

"You're forgetting I grew up in these parts."

"What's the longest you've ever walked in one day with a full ruck?" she said, standing with her hands on her hips and chin up.

"That'd be during SF selection when I did 39 miles in one night."

She grinned. "Forty-two miles in one night in Tunisia after escaping with a hostage we freed."

"How long have you gone without water in the heat while on an extended op?" he said, folding his arms across his chest.

Dev looked up at the stars, mulling over the answer. "Hmm…I'd say around sixteen hours along the Somali coast."

"Pfff…was that moving or at rest?"

"We were in a lay-up position the entire time but it was around 118 degrees during the day."

"Shit, there you go. I once did eleven hours without any water in triple-digit heat while on a mission with the Kurds."

"Well, it looks like we both get admission to the mutual admiration club—now can we get moving?"

As they continued walking along the rocky terrain, their banter continued with each trying to outdo the other until their mouths grew dry. Mitch shared some of his scant water and then finished off the last mouthful.

"We'll stick with the Apache method of clinging to the mesa rim in case we need to drop below for concealment. Hopefully we'll hit a cattle trough or rock-pocket of water somewhere. Otherwise, just put a small pebble under your tongue. It won't relieve dehydration but it will help with cottonmouth which helps with one's attitude."

"My attitude will greatly improve once we get out of this furnace."

As they walked, Dev thought about how Mitch was another mystery associated with her father's old life. In the four years she had spent learning Anatoly's tradecraft and working for his company, she felt like she still knew so little about him. The intermittent family dinners of her youth when Anatoly was home in between missions along with the stories she'd gleaned from her mother made her ache for the lost time when she needed her father the most as an adolescent.

Hearing Mitch talk about Anatoly made her realize the impact her father had had upon his life and countless others but it only filled her with envy over the vanished years she could never reclaim. She wasn't alone in her experience—most of her childhood friends with fathers in the military had the same story but it didn't make turning the anguish-filled pages of that book any easier. In the ensuing years since she began working for her father, their relationship had transmogrified into a teacher-pupil arrangement under his stern direction.

Occasionally, they both let their guards down enough to allow the old familial sentiments to bleed through but only as long as Anatoly allowed it. Dev was constantly torn between wanting to please him and her desire to simply be the best operative in the organization, given her competitive nature. At the end of the work day, all that mattered was that she was in closer proximity to her father than she had been all of her childhood, one more reason she had longed to end her assignment in the crucible of Aeneid and return to Israel.

THE FIRST SIX miles were uneventful as they traversed more boulder fields while trying to avoid wrenching an ankle or getting jabbed by the desert flora which all seemed to be designed to poke, pierce, stab, or impale.

With only a few hours of travel under their belts, Mitch was feeling the effects of physical exertion in the ninety-degree heat coupled with lack of fluid intake; his head was pounding and it seemed like every cell in his body was screaming for water. He knew Dev had to be feeling it as well but she never complained nor slowed her pace. She reminded him of some of the female ranch hands he'd grown up around that worked their tails to the bone each day in all manner of weather and got the job done no matter how brutal the field conditions. Though he'd known her less than a day, she had proven to be tough and resourceful. He still wasn't sure what would happen once they reached civilization but he admired her physical prowess and staunch independence.

As they rounded the bend in the boulder field, Mitch caught the slight glimmer of movement a mile ahead in the faint moonlight. He could make out the metallic surface of a small vehicle weaving its way along a tumbleweed-choked dirt road to the east. He motioned for Dev to stop and they secreted themselves against a vertical slab of sandstone that resembled a whale fin emanating from the desert floor.

They watched the vehicle for a few minutes until it came to a stop near a windmill. They could see two men climbing out of the open-top jeep.

"Those probably aren't cowboys out inspecting their cattle, eh," she whispered.

"Driving at midnight without their lights on? Not likely. I'm betting they're equipped with some nightvision though."

"Two of them—it'd be an even match."

He looked at her with his eyebrows raised. "You're not one to run from a fight, are you?" He glanced back towards the men, watching them as the two strode about the windmill searching for any signs on the ground.

"They know we are going to be drawn to the waterholes in the area so they're scouring those sites for potential tracks. That's what I'd do too if I were a searcher."

He chewed on his lower lip, mulling over their options. "The thing is...if we take them out, that's going to leave lots of tracks and alert the other Neanderthals that two of their guys are missing when they don't radio in."

"Then why not wait until they're done and check back in then hit them on the road on their way back out?"

He analyzed the ramifications of her plan and studied the terrain ahead of them near the single dirt road that led up the mesa. "Not a bad plan—pretty tactically sound and it puts the element of surprise in our hands. Lord knows we could sure even the odds more with their NVGs."

"Growing up in Israel, your mindset for attacks and ambushes in daily life is a given, not like over here. Just walking to school when I was a kid was exhausting because you're scanning everyone around you as a potential terrorist. It's something you can never turn off."

Though Mitch had spent his adolescence on his uncle's working cattle ranch and had a much different childhood than Dev, he knew the debilitating effects of PTSD. The daily hypervigilance that combat provided was one you could never seem to shake once you returned to civilian life. Your trust in your fellow man, outside of one's tac-team, dwindled until you saw everyone as a suspect in what felt like a conspiracy against your own sanity.

He pointed to a shadowy formation two hundred yards

away. "We can use that low outcropping of rocks to spring the ambush."

She nodded and then followed him out from behind the immense slab. They skulked around the waist-high stands of cactus then darted between the lone mesquite trees until they were beside the overgrown two-track that the jeep had driven in on. Unspooling the barbed wire he had retrieved earlier, he handed her one end as they wound it at chest-level between the tree trunks.

"Won't they see this? There's not much to conceal it," she said.

"Exactly—a good mantrap always operates on two levels, with one serving as a decoy up high to draw visual attention from the main trap on the ground or, in our case, our ambush location to their rear. I want their NVGs to pick up the barbed wire about twenty feet away so they are distracted from the chokepoint we just drew them into—that's the place where we'll attack," he said, pointing to a cluster of mesquite trees along a bend in the road."

"I'm afraid that I've mostly done urban ops over the years and don't know all this hillbilly survival stuff."

"You mean redneck—*hillbillies* are inbred country music-lovers back in the tick-infested mountains of Virginia and other backwards eastern states. We westerners use the term redneck."

She rolled her eyes. "Whatever."

Mitch kept an eye on the distant outlines of the shadowy figures near the windmill as he left Dev to finish securing the barbed wire diversion. He moved along the side of the road, being careful to step on rocks to obscure his boot prints. He moved to the curve in the road which would help to block any disturbance once the men made the turn. Instead, they would immediately be drawn to the barbed wire strung up at chest level and provide the critical seconds for Mitch and Dev to strike.

As he finished scrutinizing the ambush location, he gritted his teeth for the attack that was about to come and hoped that Dev was as fierce as she seemed. After she moved up to his location, he heard the faint call of the men radioing in their position followed by the sound of the jeep starting. He could see the vehicle undulating along the bumpy two-track towards their location. Dev and Mitch crept into the shadows by the mesquite grove ten feet from the chokepoint. Each of them readied their firearms, their throats growing further parched, as if they'd just swallowed hot coals.

17

THEY NEEDED to dispatch both guards just after the tight bend in the road where the vehicle would be moving the slowest. This would afford them a better chance of securing it before a crash occurred.

Dev was kneeling on one leg a few feet from him to the right of the road, her pistol clutched close to her chest. They were hidden behind a twelve-foot-high boulder with a polished surface, as if a giant tawny marble had sprung from the ground. The sound of the jeep's tires crunched over loose rock and the faint aroma of barrel cactus flowers wafted along the mesa.

Moving along a snaky section of the road, fifty yards away from them, the jeep jumbled along the uneven road, both men inside resembling bobble heads.

"Headshots, if possible. I don't want the jeep console damaged," said Mitch, who cast a questioning glance at her. "You sure you can do this?"

"Don't worry about me."

At the bend in the road twenty yards distant, as the driver slowed to accommodate the turn and both men noticed the barbed wire stretched between the trees, Mitch swiftly delivered both headshots, spraying the remains of the two men over the windshield. The jeep continued its forward momentum on the road as he ran alongside the open driver's side and yanked the dead man out. He hopped in, slamming on the brakes while doing a hasty check of the slumped figure next to him, whose NVGs were slightly damaged but still intact.

Dev moved alongside the rig and pulled the man in the passenger's seat out by his vest, dropping him onto the sand. "What the hell is your problem? I told you I could do it."

"Yeah, well I couldn't take the chance that you'd hesitate. You're the one that told me a while back how you weren't cut out for killing somebody in cold blood."

She just ground her teeth and growled out a deep breath. "I will do what needs to be done if the situation calls for it."

"We've got the jeep now, which is what matters, so grab anything of value off that dude and let's get rolling."

They quickly removed the body armor, weapons, ammo, and radios then continued driving over the mesa, skirting around the barbed wire. As they drove along the rock-strewn road, bobbing along in the jeep with their knees smacking the bottom of the blood-soaked dashboard, Mitch kept an eye on the massive storm clouds to the north. The spider web bolts of lightning illuminated the vapor leviathan. In between blasts of light, he saw that rain was coming down in sheets a few miles to his right. Even though the countryside around him was parched, he'd witnessed enough flash floods in the desert to know that the raging torrent of waters can come from twenty miles up canyon even if it's sunny and bone dry where you're standing.

They sped downhill for a mile past the first ravine,

which had only marginal amounts of fresh water in the puddles lining its bottom from rainfall the night before. Mitch stopped and quickly filled up their water bottles with the murky fluid, then continued driving northwest. Skirting up onto a small mesa, he continued gunning the jeep along a narrow stretch of the road that hugged the rim until it went down again. They had already covered six miles since procuring the jeep but as he crested the bend in the road and descended, he could see the moonlight reflecting off a current of coffee-colored water raging through the arroyo below. The thick brown sludge was filled with car-sized boulders and tree branches that churned like a cement mixer.

Mitch brought the jeep to a screeching halt twenty yards away from the torrent and put it in park. He climbed out and scanned the furious waters. Rubbing the back of his neck and exhaling, he punted a small stone into the current then stepped back towards the door.

"No way we can cross this—probably fifteen feet deep at least. We either sit it out here, hoping the water level goes down in the next few hours, or we trek parallel to the canyon until we find a crossing point. That could be a half-mile from here or ten miles."

Dev was already craning her head out of the window, studying the scene, then she reached into the back seat and withdrew her small pack. "I'm not staying put here. Looks like we're back to boot power."

Mitch nodded in agreement, grabbing the rest of his gear and his rifle then motioning to her to head up to the canyon rim forty feet above. "I'll be right up," he said, handing his items off to her. "I hate to foul up the desert like this but it's better to remove any evidence we came this way." Mitch went back to the jeep, removed the emergency brake and placed the stick in neutral. The vehicle rolled forward into the tumult, turning sideways upon impact with the current and joining the rest of the debris washing downstream.

He rejoined Dev, both of them watching in fascination as their brief reminder of civilization melded into the grip of the hungry waters. "The coming rains will wash away our tire tracks on the road," he said, looking north at the cumulonimbus cloud that hung upon them like a black veil. "Hopefully we can find a way across the canyon quickly and then hole up somewhere. This storm is going to be savage."

Shouldering their gear, they hoofed along the rim while scanning each small rock or cow pie to make sure it wasn't a rattler. The landscape was rife with large juniper trees and clumps of mesquite. Mitch thought for a second about how this would be good terrain for mule deer hunting and then realized how the tables were turned and they had become the prey. With the full moon in the cloudless sky at their backs and the electrical storm filling the horizon to the front, he caught a glimpse of a primitive sheepherder's bridge atop the canyon a mile up.

He tapped Dev on the shoulder and pointed to it. "Let's hope those sheepmen have been keeping that crossing point maintained."

"Why is that even there when the road isn't that far back?"

"A lot of the cattle and sheep bridges out west were put in fifty years ago or more while some of these roads came into being in the past coupla years. The ranchers prefer staying off the beaten path anyway."

His voice was drowned out as the wind shifted and began pelting them with rainfall. They picked up their pace, trotting to reach the bridge as the tempo of the storm increased with each step. Mitch could hear the current in the canyon below pulsing as if it was a living creature that would reach an arm up over the edge to claim any terrestrial being that defied it.

The moonlight was fading as the storm overtook them, the inky black clouds occasionally belting out another shockwave of lightning and thunder. *Just where I want to be right now—out in the open, near water, with the sky gods pissed off.* The last volley of lightning revealed the bridge a hundred yards out. Mitch and Dev began sprinting, crunching over ankle-high cacti in a frenzied dash to the bridge.

Making it to the edge where metal was married to rock, Mitch did a hasty inspection of the rickety contraption in between lightning flashes from above. The canyon below had swollen further and the water level was coursing four feet away from the cable suspensions that spanned the short distance between rims.

"You sure this redneck piece of shit is going to hold us?" yelled Dev.

"If not, I'll see you in Mexico," he shouted back, then grabbed the railings of spun cable on either side and began moving across. He steadied himself with the waist-high supports while half trotting, half shuffling across the creaky planks, hoping his trust in cowboy engineering wouldn't prove him wrong.

18

The raging current of mud and churning boulders below resembled a brown python undulating through the bedrock, reshaping the very walls of the canyon with its violent passing. The pounding rain was slapping against his entire body like it was trying to drive him into the hungry mouth of the silty beast below.

Mitch wanted to look over his shoulder to check on Dev but he needed every ounce of concentration upon his slippery footing and the faint contours of the approaching rim. The lightning had temporarily ceased and he had to use his boots as probes to feel for the end of the bridge. Arriving at the opposite side, he released his comforting grip on the slick cables and took a shuffle of faith into the darkness, his soles making contact with the sandstone.

He turned and stared into the inky abyss, searching for Dev. *She should've been right on my tail. Shit!* His heart rate sped further as his eyes tore through the darkness, searching for her, the squall of rain allowing only a few feet of visibility when lightning struck. He barely knew her but felt a twang of camaraderie with her given their shared connection to Anatoly and the world they operated in. She was a rare blend of elements and he had to force away the image of intrigue she presented, reminding himself that if she was gone then all of today was for nothing.

Like a specter emerging from the dark grip of the storm itself, Dev appeared in a flash of lightning, startling Mitch, who was about to retrace his precarious route. He reached forward, grabbing her arm, steadying her until they were both off the bridge. She nodded in appreciation, her face ashen as she tried to steady her wobbly legs.

"We walk side by side from here so we don't lose each other," he shouted above the roar of the canyon. "I saw some big juniper trees over this way," he said, pointing over his shoulder. "We'll head there and hole up for a few minutes."

They trudged onward, sinking at times into the goopy amalgamation of sand and pebbles that divided the panels of slickrock. Mitch paused a few times to wait for lightning illumination to get his bearings. Making it to the cluster of six massive junipers, they crawled under the thick conifers, getting some respite from the sheets of rain still scouring the land.

Mitch dropped his pack and sat down on the thick layer of duff, emitting a shriek. "Dammit," he yelled, feeling the piercing sensation of cactus spines in his palm.

"Ooh, that's not good," said Dev, inspecting the ground around her. "But better you than me."

"Very funny. How about you go find another grove of trees." He searched his palm for the spines. Dev sidled up next to him and grabbed his hand, removing the stickers with a quick tug. "I was kidding, Agent Kearns."

"Mitch will do." He winced slightly with each removal. Leaning closer, he noticed the pleasant fragrance of her hair. Since his divorce two years ago, his dating life had been non-existent by choice and he had caught himself staring at her athletic figure on more than one occasion. Now here he was being hunted in the wilds during a raging storm with a woman of considerable character and stunning features, and he was having his hand groomed. He remembered she was the daughter of his old mentor and, out of respect and reminding himself of the uncertainty of her future, he yanked his hand back. "Thanks, that feels better."

He sat up in a half-squat and looked out at the storm cell, which had begun moving to the west, the rain overhead slightly decreasing. He retrieved the compass from his pack and then moved out from under the cusp of the juniper slightly to spy a landmark. With the next lightning flash, he focused on a distant butte to the west then dialed in the bearing on his compass. "I sure as hell wouldn't mind holing up here for a few hours but we need to push on. I'd say it's only about nine miles to the interstate."

He grabbed his pack and removed a headlamp from a side pouch, flicking on the red light feature. He had maintained light discipline up to this point but needed to focus on the bearing to walk a straight line to the butte. The red light would enable him to have a low visibility tool for glancing down at the compass and avoiding falling into any crevices. He also removed the night-vision goggles from the pack that he had obtained from the driver of the jeep, waiting for the time when the lightning had passed and he could employ the device. They filed out from under the trees and trekked into the night, the storm clouds roiling off behind them and the thunder growing more distant with each step.

19

Six miles to the south, on a parched butte, Drake was leaning his shoulder against a large boulder to stabilize his vision as he scoured the landscape below with a night-vision scope on his suppressed .300 Win-Mag rifle. Time was still on their side as sunrise was nearly seven hours away and their night-vision capabilities and drones would facilitate the capture of their prey. Having worked protection details on Ritter's oil platforms in the jungles of South America, he preferred the open terrain of the desert which allowed for long-distance surveillance. It was far easier to pick up a person's movement miles away in this land of sandstone than in the dense canopy of the tropics.

Even the heat felt less intense with the lack of debilitating humidity. Drake had entertained the idea of buying a small retreat outside of Joshua Tree where he could go to unwind during his rare down time away from Aeneid. Most of his colleagues in the mercenary industry that were still alive opted for blowing their contractor pay on brothels and gambling in Thailand, spending six months relishing the cheap pleasures and then finding work again to start the cycle all over. Drake had had his fill of that life in younger days. When he sought the company of a woman, he would request one of the escort girls that Aeneid kept on speed-dial for their visiting executives.

Drake's pastime interests revolved around fine-tuning racing motorcycles. He had a collection of eleven bikes stored in the secure workshop below his loft in Fullerton, compliments of Nelson Ritter. Ritter provided him with whatever expenses were required to handle his security and excise anything that threatened to tarnish Aeneid's reputation.

This particular kill mission would allow him to have the funds to purchase a rare Indian motorcycle of which there were fewer than fifty left intact. He didn't plan on riding it, he just wanted it to round out his collection.

Schiff, one of his more experienced henchmen, came up beside him, still deferring to him instead of Perry for his orders. "We should have the portable drones up within the next few minutes. They aren't functioning well out here with the electrical storm but we should be able to pinpoint their location."

"Good, good," he said slowly as he tilted his rifle to the left, focusing on something he saw moving over a ridgeline a half-mile away.

"What is it?" said Schiff, lifting his own rifle to study the terrain where Drake was focused.

The dull *thunk* of the suppressor lasted only a microsecond. Then Drake studied the lifeless mountain lion whose front shoulder was nearly obliterated from the ballistic round.

"Never bagged me a big cat before. Shot about everything else—even a sleeping gazelle in a rich fucker's private zoo outside of Vegas—but never a mountain lion." He lowered his rifle to the ground and leaned it against the boulder. Then he tilted the brim of his cap up while grinning. "Cats are just rare as hell in the desert. This is starting out to be a good night after all."

Perry came up behind Drake and tapped his meaty shoulder. "Hey, ape-man, did you forget about not drawing attention to our location here?"

Drake turned, his lips pulled back against his teeth, which he was grinding. "This is my operation. I don't recall the boss putting you in charge of anything except giving us the location of the girl with your facial recognition software and tracking the bitch."

He moved inches away from Perry while opening his vest to reveal the hilt of his pistol. Perry swiftly reached forward, yanking the man's weapon from its holster and smacking him with the butt across the nose. Drake backpedaled, thrusting both hands up to his broken beak, which began leaking blood onto the sand.

Perry held the pistol up towards him. "You know some people just take for granted the ability to breathe clearly."

Perry heard the voice of one of the men back by the vehicles who was manipulating the drone controls. "Hey, it looks like two of our guys up on the mesa are out of commission."

Perry rushed back to the rear of the jeep, tucking the pistol in his waistline while the injured brute slowly meandered over, cursing and wiping the blood off his mouth with a bandanna. Perry studied the green laptop screen, noting the inanimate figures that were splayed on the rocky ground, their bodies not showing any heat signature.

"They checked in with me about sixty minutes ago so it shouldn't be hard to triangulate the whereabouts of their jeep." He tapped his thick finger on the screen, indicating an area to the north that had just been overtaken by a fierce thunderstorm, the black tentacles of the rain images streaking across the green monitor.

"Focus all efforts and teams on everything between that mesa and the interstate. The noose just started to close."

Perry grabbed his rifle and placed it inside his vehicle then motioned for the other five men to accompany him while the remaining three would stay behind to man the drones and mobile command center. "Ape-man, you're driving so I can study the ground," he said, tossing the keys to Drake.

As they drove down the jarring dirt road that led off the ridge, Perry scanned the terrain ahead with his night-vision goggles.

Driving by the area where the mangled corpse of the mountain lion rested, Perry focused his attention forward on the mesa in the distance and hoped he would have his captives in hand by midnight without losing any more men or being sidetracked by the impending weather. He didn't need bodies scattered all over the desert and more cover stories to fabricate. The woman was all that mattered. As for Mitch, he would cross that chasm when he came to it. *Why did he have to be tied up in all of this? He would have made a good wingman if I'd become bureau chief. Maybe he would've even come on board with my outfit once I left this God-forsaken country.* Perry shrugged his shoulders. *Then again, he's too much of a fucking throwback with his cowboy code of ethics. You were born two centuries too late, my friend.*

Perry could see the horizon ahead getting darker and heard a few raindrops pelting the windshield. He looked at the drone image on his laptop screen again as the jeep bobbed along the rocky pathway, noticing that the road coming off the mesa wound over several drainages which would serve as natural chokepoints for an ambush.

The rain began coming down in small drops at first, followed seconds later by sheets of water. Drake increased the pace, climbing out of the mucky canyon bottom until he leveled out on the mesa. Four miles further, the rain had intensified, swelling the arroyos in the region and putting a halt to their progress. Perry knew they wouldn't be making any more mileage and the drones had already gone offline, probably pulverized against the rocks somewhere.

He motioned to Drake to pull over near the canyon rim. The rain was pummeling the jeep so hard he had to shout at the men in the vehicle. "Each of you, out—set up a perimeter and keep an eye out below when this storm clears."

All of the bruisers looked at him and then at the pelting rain on the windows before climbing out into the squall. "You too, ape-man," he said to Drake. "The cold will help that broken snout of yours."

Drake slammed the door and disappeared into the downpour. Perry knew a perimeter was of little use and the men wouldn't be able to see more than twenty feet but he also didn't want to spend the next hour holed up in the tight confines of the jeep with a bunch of sweaty thugs he'd grown to despise. He wasn't like them—mercenaries. He kept telling himself that throughout the night as he studied the path of the storm on his laptop screen and waited for sunrise.

20

The first plum-colored fingers of dawn were stabbing through the clouds as Dev and Mitch climbed halfway up a small butte. It would be easier to go around it but quicker to scurry up and down the other side if they could maintain their same pace. Stopping at a knee-high pile of scree twenty yards from the rim, Dev removed her encrypted cellphone from her shoulder bag and powered it on. Mitch squatted beside her and swept the narrow dirt road below with his rifle scope. He was exhausted but they were almost at their destination and the sound of traffic blaring along the interstate was within earshot.

A few minutes later, there was an incoming text. Dev sighed and hastily typed back a reply.

"Besides a cup of coffee, I could use some good news this morning—whatcha got?" Mitch said.

"A support team of mine is inbound along the interstate. They are tracking my phone now and it looks like they'll be at the bridge there in thirty minutes," she said, pointing at a two-lane overpass about a mile away.

"God, I've driven over that bridge a thousand times.

Never thought I'd be racing to reach it on foot from this side."

Between their location and their exfil location were hundreds of acres of thick cactus and cholla. He was about to suggest a route when the trunk of a large mesquite tree splintered into pieces, sending a shower of woodchips to his feet. He ducked beneath the rocks, trying to identify where the rifle shot had come from as another round impacted the slab in front of him.

Dev was crouching low beside Mitch, peering through a crevice in the rockpile. "They're down in the ravine along the road, about a half-mile away—maybe four or more guys."

Mitch craned his head up at the ridgeline behind them. "We need to get up and over then make an all-out sprint for the interstate. Go first and I'll cover you."

"I can cover you," she snapped back.

"You think your sharpshooting skills are superior to mine?" he barked.

"We're wasting time, now go."

He grabbed her arm as Dev was about to position the M4 he'd given her. "My weapon can reach out farther than yours so get your ass over that ridge," he said, patting the stock of the scoped Remington 700 rifle in his clutches.

"Pfff," she mumbled while getting in place to scurry up the butte. Mitch let loose a volley of rounds into the region below where he'd located several muzzle blasts. After his sixth shot, Dev was out of sight.

Another barrage of machinegun fire ricocheted off the surrounding rocks near his head as he reloaded his weapon. He got on his elbows and moved eight feet over to a different opening in the rock cavity. With the gunfire below ceasing, Mitch resumed shooting off more rounds and then spun, kicking loose the foundation of the scree to create a small rockslide, then began his sprint up the incline. The boulders around him were shattering from incoming shots and he felt his legs being pelted by rock shrapnel while the twang of ricochets echoed off the slabs.

As he cleared the ridge and ran out of sight of the shooters below, Dev was nowhere to be seen. The compressed rocks on the ground indicated her direction of travel and he followed those for fifty feet until he saw her squatting in the shade of a tree, her weapon fixed on the road below. Upon his arrival, she began walking in a zig-zag pattern down the side as he followed a few feet behind, keeping his eyes on her hands.

"I was wondering where the hell you went. I was hoping it wasn't to hitch a ride without me," Mitch said, knowing that he had bought them some time with the rockslide, which would temporarily block the road.

"Why would I do such a thing? That's not how I work."

"I barely know you, lady. You needed me to get you across the desert and now you're nearly home free with your buds on the way. How do I know that they're not gonna give me a dirt nap when we reach the vehicle?"

"You are a trusted friend of my father's. That's why he sent me to you in the first place. Besides, you are a skilled warrior and I am in need of such help."

As she turned sideways to face him, he studied her face for a moment but her hardened expression left no room for interpreting if what she was saying was true. His gut feelings told him to continue forward with her but he was reluctant to take her at her word. "Just stay close to me."

"You're right, you don't know me. You could have shot me back at the ranch when I was on your porch or you could've left me in the desert and walked out to save your own hide but you didn't." She stood still and gave him a hard stare. "Why not?"

He was growing irritated with her as her questions prodded at the veneer of allegiance he felt towards his job as a federal agent. "When I find out, I'll let you know, believe me. Now let's push on. There's only the one dirt road around this butte and those guys will find a way to get back on task."

Once they reached more level ground where the butte and valley below met, they began trotting through the gnarly terrain, frequently glancing over their shoulders as the two-lane bridge grew closer in their vision. The roar of vehicles on the interstate echoed off the valley and he knew they had only minutes to make it off the exposed terrain to the ravine beneath the bridge.

Dev glanced at her Smartphone again while continuing to jog. "Extraction in seven minutes. This is going to be a close one."

This endurance run reminded Mitch of his SERE course at Fort Bragg where he underwent a five-day survival and evasion trek while being pursued by civilians bent on his capture. The students who lasted the longest were the ones who possessed above-average aerobic capacity and could simply outrun the "hostiles." Only then there weren't armed mercenaries sending rounds downrange and a mysterious woman for a companion. He detested the former and still wasn't sure how he felt about the latter.

21

"We just have to hold them off a little while longer," Dev said, looking at her cellphone again.

With the sun above the horizon, Mitch could make out the approaching jeeps driven by the hostiles through the scope on his sniper rifle. They were heading along the winding dirt road that skirted below the rim about two miles distant.

"I'll drive a few rounds through the engine blocks as soon as they're in range," he said, adjusting the elevation and windage dials on the scope then racking a .308 round into the chamber. He scanned the nearby terrain for a landmark that was approximately 800 yards out. Spying the upright skeleton of a dead saguaro cactus near the road, he locked it in on his mental map and prepared for the shot. He welded his cheek to the rifle stock and then began pacing his breathing, falling into a four-count rhythm.

As the lead vehicle rounded the last bend in the canyon, he zoomed in on the tan grille. Waiting until the jeep was directly under the saguaro, he fired a single round into the front then racked another round and fired at the second vehicle. Both came crashing to an immediate halt, slamming into patches of knee-high cholla that littered the dirt shoulder.

He refocused his attention on the men scrambling out of the lead vehicle and lined up the crosshairs on the front passenger, who had disembarked. Mitch blinked hard and gulped down a breath. *What the fuck?* He squinted into the reticle and stared at the face of Perry, who was barking orders at the other men running behind nearby boulders. He pulled back for a second, shaking his head, then refocused his gaze to be sure of what he saw. *Perry is in on this!* He swallowed hard and then yelled back to Dev, who was covering the area towards the interstate.

"That contact you traced to Phoenix? What was the name?"

She hesitated and then blurted it out. "Kovac—Perry Kovac. At least, he's the one I suspected of being Aeneid's inside man."

"How the hell can this be?" he muttered, taking his finger off the trigger and balling his fist.

"Does that name ring a bell?"

Mitch didn't answer and only clenched his jaw, trying to clear his mind enough to focus on the scene in his sight. He saw the men dispersing amongst the boulders and flowing along the side of the road. They split into two teams, with one hugging the terrain near the road while Perry's group darted cross-country along an old rockslide which provided ample concealment.

Mitch swung his rifle back to the other group opposite Perry's location. Picking out a rail-thin goon darting from tree to tree, he shot the man clear through the sternum, dropping him back onto a fallen log. This caused the man in front to pause long enough for Mitch to drive a round through his upper left pectoral, obliterating most of the shoulder joint, which caused the arm to dangle like a rotting tree branch in the wind.

The rest of the men took cover behind boulders or cottonwood trees. Mitch shifted his attention back to Perry's group, catching his colleague in the crosshairs. Perry was close enough now that the scope revealed his tan face and square jaw. Mitch eased off the trigger for a second and took a deep breath. *You son of a bitch.* He fired a round onto the boulder beside Perry, spraying rock shrapnel up into the man's face. He saw Perry drop back, clutching his cheek, and then he disappeared behind a dead tree trunk. *We're not done here. I need your ass alive.*

The other mercenaries were out of sight below the second ridgeline where Mitch was perched. He crawled backwards with his rifle, making it to Dev's location on the other side of the hill. Six hundred yards away was the interstate, its ribbon of traffic relatively light for a Monday morning.

"Perry Kovac—what did you have on him? What was his involvement in all of this again?"

"He has to be the one manipulating security footage and surveillance for the weapons to arrive here. All I know from the file I scanned is that the attacks are connected with Iranian terrorists or some proxy group."

"That's beyond even Perry's clearance level."

"Then he's got someone like Monroe or someone higher up in D.C. pulling the strings. That's the part I don't have yet but it's all here on this flash drive," she said, patting her hand against her shirt pocket.

Mitch looked down at the interstate. "So, we're just gonna run up to the white line on the blacktop and leap in when your pals come, eh? Is that the plan?" Mitch said, keeping his eyes focused in the direction of Perry and his men.

"You said you were a cowboy, right? I would've thought that that plan would suit you just fine."

Fifty yards from the overpass, Mitch stopped and perched beside a fallen logjam of debris that was wedged under the steel girders of the bridge. He knew Perry and his men would be attacking them in an all-out effort to prevent their escape. Mitch just hoped that there would be no collateral damage above from motorists speeding along the interstate—that they would drive by never knowing the struggle for survival that was unfolding below them. How he envied them in this moment, with their faces pressed into a map of the Grand Canyon.

His mind shifted back to the drainage. There was a slight hint of a blond orb poking out from a cluster of tamarisk trees to the right. Mitch readied his rifle, waiting for a glimmer of confirmation on his target. A second later, the hulking brute's head split apart, the skullcap flying off like a swift breeze had plucked it free. He heard Dev cycle another round into her rifle, surprised that she had beaten him to the shot but grateful for her marksmanship.

"That was Drake—a sniveling, disgusting son of a bitch who was Aeneid's head of security."

Mitch heard the screech of tires on the overpass. "Let's go," he said.

They used bounding moves to cover each other as they snaked their way up the concrete embankment to the guardrails until they were at the confluence of desert and interstate where a white SUV had just come to a stop. The passenger-side doors swung open, the faces of several dark-skinned men revealing themselves. Dev leapt into the front seat while Mitch paused for a second, unsure of what came next but knowing it had to be better than the alternative of remaining below. He climbed in, the rail-thin man taking Mitch's rifle while the SUV sped off as quickly as it had arrived.

Mitch gulped in a deep breath, scanning the canyon below for any signs of Perry and his goons until they were clear of the region. He swung his head around to the driver, catching the cunningly familiar eyes in the rearview mirror of Anatoly Leitner.

22

The vehicle sped north along I-17, hovering just over the speed limit. Mitch looked over the crew around him and then sank back into the seat, feeling the blast of air-conditioning flowing over him.

He peered ahead at the driver. For a man in his mid-sixties, who had endured a lifetime of combat, Anatoly was still remarkably fit. His massive calloused hands that resembled baseball mitts seemed mismatched with his lanky six-foot-two frame. Mitch had once heard from a fellow colleague of Anatoly's that the man had over two dozen knife and bullet wounds on his body, though the stone-faced old warrior rarely spoke of his exploits. Despite this, the man looked like a grandfatherly figure who'd be more at home mowing the lawn than executing rescue missions in third-world hotspots.

Mitch could see the resemblance between father and daughter. Same rounded chin, slender nose, and those riveting brown eyes that could flare up in intensity, letting you know that you just fucked with the wrong person.

Dev and Anatoly began conversing in Hebrew,

exchanging information on the events of the past few days since Dev left California. The other men were silent, scanning the terrain ahead like hawks bent on procuring a rabbit. The stout man beside Mitch had a caterpillar-like mustache that hung over his upper lip. The other one had a boyish, clean-cut face that resembled a college kid, though his scarred knuckles and furrowed hands indicated otherwise.

When father and daughter were done, Anatoly swiveled slightly in his seat and glanced at Mitch. "Good to see you, old friend. It's been a long time. I am grateful for what you did to help Devorah."

"Not as grateful as I'll be when you tell me exactly what is going on and how you're gonna make this right—I mean the fleeing-from-a-federal-manhunt part not the part about leading a small army of thugs to my buddy's ranch, causing us to be hunted for two days."

"We have much to talk about, it seems." There was a long pause, as if the older man was leaving an opening in the conversation for Mitch to respond.

"So, Anatoly, maybe you can answer me this: your daughter tells me that you never got out of the game after you left the States," Mitch said, still sore that the man had never kept in touch with him despite numerous attempts on Mitch's part.

"There's a place in Jordan called "The Tunnel of Souls," said Anatoly, who never seemed to answer a question directly and had to relay a story. It had always irritated the hell out of Mitch but he had grown accustomed to it. The man continued, his eyes focused intently on the road but his mind drifting to another place. "This tunnel leads to the netherworld and requires that you pay with four years of your life here on Earth in order to have one day in purgatory having your questions answered."

He looked at Mitch, casting a slight grin. "After I left here, I went into a partnership with several old Mossad colleagues. Together we focused on rescuing others from hellish dictatorships around the globe and building a trusted network of informants, particularly in Turkmenistan. It took me years of diligence...of patience...of the blood of my associates to unravel what you are now tied up in." Anatoly glanced at the mountains in the distance. "Surely you must remember what it was like dipping your fingers into the covert world—where every alliance is to be questioned and where the man watching your back for years has just accepted an offer from a rival and wants you dead. Your government job couldn't have driven those memories completely out of you."

"You seemed to always fare better in that world than I did. Besides, I was in army special operations, not clandestine, off-the-books missions with some unaccountable shadow agency. There's a big difference."

"Both approaches are just tools for excising the cancer that grows in other nations opposed to our respective governments' agendas. Your unit's actions may have been more transparent and the after-effects observable but the end goal was the same as what I did: stabilizing or destabilizing regions to further Western might."

"You always did have a way of putting things into a certain perspective. I left the military because our operational policies were starting to get a little too gray for me. I prefer a more black-and-white world."

"Those days are gone, my friend. The modern world of global warfare is a sepulcher of half-truths driven by monetized agendas. Actually that's not too different than warfare during any other time but now the currency is the welfare of entire nations versus just a cart full of gold or silk."

"Yeah, well the way I see it, a soldier still has a choice in whether he buys into the system."

Anatoly chuckled. "Aren't you with the FBI—the very bastion of American self-righteousness?"

Mitch leaned his arms forward on his knees, glancing at the older man. "That's right, and doing a damn fine job at upholding the law," he said, trying to put force into the latter half of his reply.

"Good for you. The bureau should be grateful to have such a dedicated warrior in its ranks."

Mitch looked at him, trying to determine if the man was being sarcastic or serious. He turned away and sighed, unsure if he'd still have any kind of job ever again after today.

The man sitting next to Mitch reached in the back seat, removing some t-shirts from a duffle bag. He handed one to Mitch and another to Dev. "Will help with blending in better, yes," said the man with a slight accent. He then introduced himself as Petra while the other fellow muttered his name in a gravelly voice as if coughing it up: "Daniel."

Mitch removed his soiled vest and then peeled off the sweaty black shirt that clung to his frame. He donned the blue t-shirt which had the expression, *I Survived the Grand Canyon* written across it with the image of boot prints heading into the sunset. He just smirked and bit his lip at the irony.

"So, you boys former Mossad too or just handpicked by Anatoly himself?"

Petra looked forward at Anatoly for his directions. After the older man nodded in approval, Petra replied, "I was Mossad for six years but then was discharged for medical injury to my shoulder. Now I work for Mr. Leitner, doing comms and intel."

The other man stroked his considerable mustache while replying as if the action of grooming conjured up his answer. "Much time in Mossad. Now do weapons training for new recruits with Mr. Leitner's organization."

Mitch glanced up front, his lips creasing outward into a partial grin. "Anatoly...it's alright if I call you Anatoly, isn't it, or should it be Mr. Leitner?"

He could see that look in Anatoly's eyes in the mirror, the familiar stare from years ago that he'd come to respect, the cauldron of fury beneath it being calmly contained. "Anatoly will do for you, my young friend, as long as I don't have to call you Agent Kearns."

23

Perry had retreated to the side of a massive logjam that had accumulated from many flash floods, the bare limbs twisted like oversized pretzels against the embankment. He gazed down at Drake's shattered skull a few feet away, the man's limp figure splayed out on the sand. The yellowjackets that had been gathered at the mud puddle a few feet away swarmed over the bone splinters and gray matter.

Perry retrieved his cellphone and called Nelson Ritter.

"Mr. Kovac, I hope this call brings good news."

"Afraid not—Sanchez got away. She had help from a federal agent."

"You said this would be a quick snatch-and-grab operation."

"Don't worry, they can't get too far but we should delay the operation."

"Not an option. There are too many dominos that have already begun to fall. The shipment of assault weapons and explosives is arriving shortly."

The situation is too volatile until we have Sanchez in our hands."

"You're not hearing me—the funds have already been moved to the key players. These are not the type of people you request a refund from." There was a long pause, Nelson's increased exhalations the only sign that he was still on the phone until he barked into Perry's ear, "Get to Anaheim, handle the exchange or you're dead. Is that clear enough for you?"

Perry grimaced and then sighed. "Crystal."

"In the meantime, what needs to be done to hunt down Sanchez and this agent she's with?"

"If she has the files you indicated, what will she need to decode them?"

Ritter was silent for a moment. "The only place to decrypt those is here at Aeneid. Our software is proprietary and our files accessible only through our company mainframe."

"Then just shut those portals down until after the attack is launched. She'll be crippled. They'll just be two fugitives on the run that will get picked up a few weeks from now at some restaurant in Denver."

"Impossible to do something on that scale without affecting all of our other internal networks which will only cause delays in the upcoming operation. However, we can make it easy for them to enter the facility, luring them inside, and then disposing of them after."

Perry thought about Mitch as he felt the searing pain in his cheek from the earlier splinters of rock shards that lacerated his face. "That should work. Just leave the FBI agent to me. And one more thing—your head brute is without a head. He was taken out by the fugitives along with seven other guys."

There was a muffled sigh from Nelson. "He's off the

books and won't show up in any databases. Pity, he was years in the making."

Perry cleared his throat as he kicked dirt onto Drake's chest. "I'll be there as soon as I make sure things are covered with my bureau chief."

"My jet will be waiting for you in Phoenix. And Perry—this had better go without any further glitches. I want the files, the woman, and these loose ends tied up by nightfall."

Perry grunted into the phone then hung up and shouted back to the remaining six men who were concealed amongst the bushes, their weapons still fixed on the canyon. "Strip ape-man of all his gear."

He started retreating back down their approach route to the disabled vehicles. "You men disperse and make your way back to Phoenix. I need to retrace my steps and emerge a few miles to the southwest. After that, I'll be in touch about the next leg of this mission."

24

His name was Fareed Mahmoud. His life growing up in the foothills of Iran had given him fortitude. His commitment to the Koran had provided a roadmap for devotion which his twisted mind had bent to match his own desires, and four years at the University of California in Los Angeles had stoked the raging fires of discontent against the infidel. His chatroom conversations in Persian with other discontented students and a later visit to a training camp in Yemen were what made Nelson Ritter smile.

Religion was of little use in Ritter's own thinking. He had long ago shucked off his formal Catholic upbringing. He surmised that one's destiny was shaped by an iron-clad will, timing, cunning, and destroying your competitors. But he did recognize religious zealotry as a powerful business tool for galvanizing his causes.

Fareed and his associates at UCLA were perfect for Ritter's small-scale attack on U.S. soil. He knew it didn't have to be spectacular, nor did there have to be a large body-count—there only had to be enough attention drawn to Fareed's Iranian heritage to rally support with outraged corporate financiers who would pull out of their oil interests in the Caspian Sea. Russia, Kazakhstan, Turkmenistan, and Azerbaijan formed a pact on the division of the Caspian Sea resources over a decade ago. Iran had been disputing that claim line, which would grant them the lion's share of 48 billion barrels of oil along trillions of cubic meters of natural gas.

Iran's involvement in a homegrown terrorist cell in the U.S. would thrust them onto the world stage, allowing Ritter's expansion efforts in neighboring Turkmenistan to proceed. With Iran out of the way, the oil would flow unobstructed through the new pipeline to Europe, placing Ritter and his colleagues into the realm of nearly unlimited power in the region and with bank accounts to match.

Fareed was smart, idealistic, and charismatic. His loose affiliations with extremist groups would serve as enough of a catalyst for the American media to run with their own versions of fabricated reality. Ritter knew that fact-checking had exited American journalism with the advent of social media, which only needed embryonic half-stories to give birth to what the masses felt like absorbing during that week's news cycle.

The other disillusioned youths in Fareed's jihadist group were spread around the Los Angeles region, most still working menial jobs to pay for their schooling. Every Wednesday evening they would meet at an abandoned car stereo warehouse on Lamson Avenue, south of downtown Anaheim. The building was owned by Fareed's uncle, who had shuttered the business with the recent economic downturn.

Each week, the group focused on a skill set revolving around dry-fire practice drills with their firearms, room clearing techniques, and studying small unit tactics that

Fareed had learned during his brief time in Yemen. Once a month, they also went out to the desert around Joshua Tree and did endurance runs with their heavily laden backpacks to simulate an evasion scenario. Though he prayed he would die in a hail of bullets after expending his weapons in a fiery battle, Fareed had also become intrigued with the survival mindset, which added another tool to his pseudo-tactical mindset.

Unknown to the others in his group, Fareed had stowed a few 10mm rocket boxes in the desert in case he was ever on the run. He obtained these from a military surplus store in Riverside. These had been buried in a GPS-marked site near Palm Springs at the base of a cliff. The cache contained enough survival gear, rations, pistol magazines, ammunition, and first-aid items for Fareed to be on the lam for a few days.

His escape route out of Los Angeles ran along the I-10 corridor skirting around Palm Springs and he had sat up many long nights plotting out what an exciting escape from justice would look like from the comfort of his laptop. After that he wasn't sure what he would do but he had read on various survival forums that an evader should always have a three-day supply of goods to "Get Out of Dodge," whatever the hell that meant.

Ritter had followed Fareed's whereabouts for the past nine months, eventually sending one of his senior mercenaries of Egyptian descent, Gamal, who feigned alliance with an Al Qaeda affiliate to build a relationship of trust in their common interests. Through many clandestine meetings, the plans for six lone-wolf attacks were made, the resolve built, the men assembled, and the targets identified. Now all that was needed was the might. Ritter was thrilled, his spine electric, when the call finally came in from Gamal that the pieces had aligned.

He made the necessary calls to Assistant Secretary of Defense Thomas Monroe and Agent Perry Kovac to ensure the incoming shipment of weapons and demolition gear would arrive without incident, the cargo plane's manifest and customs requirements being reassigned to another vessel. The AK-47s would then be meticulously stamped on the metal receiver above the handguard with the symbol of the Iranian flag. Ritter saw to it that his personal team of mercenaries handled the crates, planting enough evidence to reveal the source was an extremist group led by Fareed with the sanction of Iranian rebels.

Everything had come to pass as he, Monroe, and Perry had painstakingly planned at Monroe's private chalet in Tahoe nearly a year ago. Ritter felt like he knew what it must be like to be an artist—the delicate brushstrokes unfolding over months until the canvas emerged into a thing of beauty that made you stand back and sigh.

THAT NIGHT in his estate in northwest Anaheim, Nelson Ritter sat on the second floor of his private office, the large French doors that led out to the porch glistening with the last rays of sunlight over the palm tree-lined pool below. The ten-thousand-square-foot mansion had nine bathrooms and six bedrooms and sat perched above the valley in a cul-de-sac, with Ritter owning the adjoining undeveloped parcels.

His office was designed to resemble that of a Roman chancellor, the walls paneled with knotty walnut and gold etchings of spear-toting men in chariots engaged in the Battle of Carthage. In the middle, a chandelier made of elk antlers hung from the hand-carved ceiling which revealed the Roman amphitheater in its former splendor. On each wall were gold-framed photographs depicting Ritter with various dignitaries, politicians, and dictators, the most notable from the latter being Surinam Presidente Eduarto del Toro, whom he helped to install in power in the '90s but then later had to have assassinated once oil reserves in that country were depleted. While the entire room fostered an electrical ambience, it had been designed by a safe-room manufacturer with two-foot-thick steel walls, a floor with a pressure-plate security system, along with bulletproof porch windows and a vault-like entrance door. Nelson worked at home on Tuesday and Wednesday, handling Aeneid's board meetings via Skype for a few hours while several Latina women lounged in his bedroom for his frequent respites throughout the day.

On his teak-lined desk, which seemed to occupy a third of the room, was a picture of Ritter clad in soiled olive-drab fatigues in the jungle bordered by two native guerrilla fighters. The youthful Ritter was grinning while clutching an Ingram Mac-10 submachine gun with a suppressor. Beside this oversized picture was a miniscule framed photograph of Ritter and his fourth wife, a woman thirty years younger and of Panamanian descent. Isabella divided her time between their villa in the Italian Alps and their Anaheim estate, which was the arrangement Ritter preferred.

The 72-inch flattop computer screen mounted to the wall across from his desk was voice activated, allowing him to dictate while keeping his hands free to sift through black-and-white reconnaissance photos of the Sangar Valley in Turkmenistan. That draconian nation was perfect for his upcoming venture as it had the second most repressive government in the world next to North Korea and was closed to independent scrutiny and outside media.

As he sat back in his leather throne chair, Ritter's thoughts floated over his recent interactions with Perry. He was eagerly awaiting a call from the man, hoping the woman had been plucked from her whereabouts and would soon be back at Aeneid for *questioning*.

Ritter had done his homework on Perry through his own surveillance work along with what he gleaned from the endless arm-candy informants that he fed the man and the constant analysis of Perry's personal finances. When the opportunity arose to present Perry with a lucrative offer for his insider services at the FBI, the two joined forces. Ritter had always kept plenty of audio recordings of their interactions and was judicious in his business meetings to provide deniability for himself while keeping just enough rope for Perry to hang himself with if things ever went askew.

The phone rang, and Ritter clumsily grabbed it in his haste to hear the news. His jaw sank when he heard a voice other than Perry's in his ear. It was Gamal, who was calling to inform him of the weapons shipment for Fareed.

"Clear?"

"Yes, this line is secure," said Gamal. "The packages have arrived and are being safeguarded until the delivery."

"Excellent. Transfer will take place within the next 48 hours. I'm waiting on one issue to resolve itself."

"Do we have a location?"

Ritter thought for a moment, his bony fingers tapping on the edge of the desk. "Let's plan on having Fareed select the spot, as long as it's safe. That'll give him a sense of ownership in the plan."

"Very well, sir. I will make the arrangements and wait for your call on the timing."

Ritter hung up the phone and stood, rubbing his sore neck. Then he walked over to a wooden cabinet and poured himself a glass of vodka. He tried to wash away the tension, pensively staring at his phone on the desk as if his searing gaze would cause it to ring.

25

Two hours later, Perry had made the arduous trek back to the canyon where his FBI colleagues had previously been ambushed. The fly-ridden corpses had been visited by vermin during the night and their noses and fingertips were gnawed away. He scratched nervously at his temple, staring at the bloated remains of the former agents and feeling like Ritter's bitch in some scheme that he was too deep to extricate himself from. He thought his role would only be providing inside intel and occasional computer data, not an accomplice in the demise of such finely trained men. *Fucking Ritter. Sitting in his lofty perch delegating orders.*

He took a deep breath, running through his cover story for the hundredth time before he radioed back to headquarters. His sunbaked fingertips were cracked and sore. He looked down at his hands, wondering what had happened to the man he was twenty-four hours ago, then his mind shifted to his lacerated face. *Fucking Mitch. He's the reason this all went south. My part would've already been over if that woman hadn't shown up at his place. How the hell is he woven into this nightmare?*

He pulled out his radio and called Ryker, noticing a few drops of blood staining his vest from busting Drake's nose mingled with his own facial injuries. He dabbed his fingers in the wet sand and scoured off the mess.

"What do you mean the trail went cold?" said the bureau chief.

"The flash floods last night wiped the area clean. I've been running on empty all day."

"Stay put. I'll send a helo out to get you and your team."

He took a deep breath. "Just me. The rest of my guys—they...they..." He paused and counted to three in his head for greater drama. "They're dead. It was Mitch, he was the shooter."

"Holy Christ! What do you mean Mitch? He gunned them down, all of them? Why would he do that?"

"The guy's gone off the reservation. He and this woman must be into some heavy shit."

"I can't believe it. Mitch is a stand-up guy from what I know. Are you sure?"

"I was there, sir. We identified ourselves and then he burned them all down right before my eyes. I barely made it out myself."

Ryker was silent, then cleared his throat. "Alright, alright...I, uhm...look, just hunker down where you are and I'll have a team inbound within thirty minutes."

An hour later Perry was sitting in the briefing room with Ryker, recounting his story and poring over the file on Mira Sanchez. The bodies of the three downed agents had been flown- out with him and were in the coroner's office two blocks away. Ryker had pulled up the computer images of

Sanchez that were pinged off the facial recognition program. It showed her at a gas station in the town of Cave Creek, eighteen miles south of the ranch.

"So, who were these mercenaries that were pursuing them—did you get a look at any of those guys?"

"No, they must have pulled out of the area after we moved in, although Mitch caught one in a mantrap and executed him. The guy's throat was slit from ear to ear." Perry simulated the motion with his thumb across his own neck.

Perry lowered his head, massaging his forehead and speaking in a low voice. "After he mowed down my team and disappeared, I followed him for a little while but knew that he may have more trail deterrents in place. I got caught in the storm that rolled through and had to hunker down in place for the night. That's why I went dark for a while."

Ryker studied Perry's face for a moment and then picked up the black-and-white photograph of Sanchez, tossing it on the table beside her work dossier from Aeneid.

"I just don't get it. Mitch teams up with her and then goes on the lam, taking out our guys. I don't know the man well but it just doesn't seem like him."

"Then why's he on the run if he's not guilty? Mitch has been bought. He's got no family, no wife, nothing in his life to keep him honorable. They must have some prior relationship and are involved in the recent corporate espionage that went down at that private contracting firm in the email you sent."

Perry stood up, resting his knuckles on the table. "If there isn't anything else, I just want to get cleaned up and have a few minutes to myself."

Ryker stopped him at the door, standing in the entry. "You know Mitch better than anyone else here. I want you to get with the rest of the tac-team in the conference room when you're done and see what you can contribute to his whereabouts—and Perry, I want him brought back alive."

"Sure." Perry just smirked then lowered his head. "I thought I knew the man. Now I'm not so sure. Maybe all of his demons finally caught up with him."

Ryker watched Perry disappear around the corner and then walked back inside the debriefing room. He stared at the image of Sanchez while picking up the phone beside him. He dialed the D.C. office and requested the international activities division. He entered his security code and badge ID.

"This is Bureau Chief Evan Ryker. I want to request an Interpol search on Mira Sanchez along with any correlation between her and FBI Agent Mitchell Kearns. We've not found anything on our internal databases on the woman and need to cast our net wider."

The agent on the other end indicated that she would get back to him within two hours, after which he hung up and resumed poring over the map of Arizona on his laptop.

26

ANATOLY DROVE the white SUV for another fifteen miles north, pulling off at a remote exit in the desert. Below the overpass was a white delivery van. Inside were two more of Anatoly's men. The man in the driver's seat, who had a trim beard, was tall enough to have to scrunch to sit comfortably. The other was younger and built like a linebacker. Mitch and Dev transferred into the vehicle while Anatoly grabbed his gear and rifle from the SUV.

"You got a clean cellphone I can use?" Mitch said to Anatoly. The older man reached into his shirt pocket and pulled out an encrypted Smartphone, passing it over.

As they resumed their trip north in one vehicle, Mitch dialed in Ryker's number at the FBI office in Phoenix. When the man picked up, Mitch didn't wait to do an overview of the past twenty-four hours, but instead cut to the chase. "This is Mitch. Perry has no doubt told you his side of the story by now."

"He said you're the shooter and took out his men. Mitch —what the hell is going on? Did you know this woman is on the FBI's Top Ten list?"

How's that possible? It takes time and a dozen bureau protocols to get bumped to the top of the list from nowhere. "Perry is a traitor. His goons killed our men and he probably led them right into the trap. He's feeding you false intel to hide his involvement with the Aeneid Corporation, which is planning a major attack inside our borders."

"What? What proof do you have?"

Mitch looked over at Dev, knowing she was the only link to his innocence and the story he was conveying. It was his word against Perry's, only Mitch was on the run, confirming his guilt with each passing mile. "When I have something more solid I'll call you," he said, the words feeling sticky in his mouth.

Mitch hung up, handing the phone back to Anatoly. He felt his stomach coiling in knots. His colleague was setting him up and with resources at his disposal that Mitch no longer had. He was alone, cut off except for the people beside him in the vehicles, whose motives he wasn't entirely clear about.

Mitch stared straight ahead at the miles of blacktop that spun by in a blur, barely noticing the desert terrain around him. "What evidence do you have, exactly?" he said to Dev. "We're not going to be able to stay in evasion mode for long. I know how these federal manhunts work, remember?"

"When we stop at our next location, I'll show you," she said. "Just stick it out with us, Mitch."

An hour and a half later, they arrived at a cabin in the mountains west of Flagstaff. It was located six miles down a secondary road and was a two-story structure made of ponderosa pine surrounded by miles of national forest.

Out of habit, Mitch scanned the ground for tracks as they got out. He could see that the place probably hadn't been used in weeks and the leaf litter on the driveway didn't show any signs of disturbance.

"A friend of yours own this?" said Mitch.

"Nah, Airbnb—great resource for travelers who want to stay anonymous," said Anatoly with a smile as they walked up to the wrap-around porch.

Mitch yanked on the pewter door handle and found it locked. "You're not gonna stay anonymous if you have to meet the owner for the keys or break in."

"The cyber division of my company, small though it is, developed an invasive software used for surveillance of civilian businesses that we sometimes need in our line of work. It tells us when places like Airbnb rentals are vacant, correlated to their calendar listings and the owner's personal Facebook pages of when they will be out of town—it's amazing what people will post to the world about their daily whereabouts."

Anatoly motioned to Petra, his second-in-command, to pick the lock and deactivate the inside alarm.

"Most of the time, we just need a house for a few hours or one night to hole up away from the city or near the staging area of a target."

Mitch saw Anatoly look around the edge of the woods, noting the defensible slopes. "We need to lie low for a bit and discuss our plans for the coming phase," said the older man.

As the front door swung open, two of Anatoly's men swept inside, clearing the abode. Anatoly proceeded in, his hand on his HK pistol, while glancing around at the glass-lined cabinets around the kitchen. "This guy better have some rum or brandy in his coffers. The last place we stayed at was some Mormon's house in central Utah and all he had was apple juice and spritzers."

Given Anatoly's reputation as a professional assassin, Mitch was always amazed at the older man's ability to go from being a stone-faced killer to a grinning joker in a flash. He also knew more filthy jokes than anyone Mitch had ever met, though those weren't likely to be part of the evening repertoire with Dev present. Then again, he thought, maybe she'd inherited those traits too.

The interior of the cabin resembled a luxury yacht more than a rustic abode. The cathedral ceiling had elk-antler chandeliers hanging from them, highlighting the spacious living room beneath, which was replete with leather couches positioned around a native-stone fireplace.

"Geez, this joint looks like it should be in Aspen, not Flagstaff," said Mitch. "Must be those Californians who built this for a third home thinking that my state is their backyard."

That afternoon, they had a simple meal of rice, beans, salsa, and tortillas along with some cognac Anatoly hunted down. With the four men taking guard duty outside, Dev and her father sat around the gas fireplace discussing the happenings at Aeneid interspersed with talk about recent events in Israel. Mitch sat in a leather recliner and took in the banter between father and daughter, his mind drifting back to his friend's ranch, where he'd shared many similar dinners around the open campfire.

Mitch saw a side of Anatoly that he had never witnessed before. His usual stolid expression was replaced by a tranquility and warmth as he spoke with Dev, his hand occasionally brushing against her arm tenderly. Mitch had always felt a sense of reverence being in the presence of such a seasoned warrior but now he was deeply moved by the untenable connection between father and daughter that permeated the cabin.

Anatoly swigged down the last of his drink then looked at Mitch. "You still look like a soldier—only it's a job as a government agent man, eh?"

Mitch gave Dev a sideways glance. "It was...until yesterday when your daughter came a-knockin'."

"She has a way of turning a person's world upside down, it seems."

Dev smiled, her face even more radiant than Mitch had noticed before.

"We should look over the files I obtained from Aeneid," she said, reaching into her soiled shoulder bag and retrieving her laptop.

"So this is where you show me the nefarious schematics for the attack and how we can thwart it, right?" said Mitch, who moved over next to Dev on the couch as the three began eagerly waiting for the device to power up.

He grew wide-eyed as he watched her insert the flash drive.

"Relax," she said, tapping her fingers on a silver device with a small antenna. "I've got my computer routing our location to six other locations around the globe so we're safe. Just like you setting up those dummy trails earlier. I had to wait until my father could provide this gadget otherwise I would've tried to do this days ago."

Dev clicked on the precious files she had risked so much to obtain. A small red warning box popped up indicating the data was inaccessible. She sighed and tried again only to have the same thing occur. After a third attempt she examined the properties of the flash drive, her eyebrows scrunching together as she slammed a fist on the table. "There's a phantom security firewall encrypting these files."

"I thought you bypassed those when you initially obtained the data," said Anatoly.

"I did—two layers of software security had to be breached. This must be something that was attached without my knowing as a result of breaking through the other layers. It's a 'Remora'—a cloaked firewall that is programmed to latch onto a file about to be hacked." She ran her fingers through her hair as her eyes widened. "This is cutting-edge technology that only a few governments in the world use. How did Aeneid get a hold of this?"

"You already know the answer," said Mitch. "This company has deep pockets that are filled by someone high up in D.C. like Monroe."

"He's right," said Anatoly. "Monroe is the foundation of this whole enterprise, though without access to that data file, it will be hard to prove."

"With your former government connections, why not just hand this intel over to our agencies here?" said Mitch, looking at Anatoly.

"'Former connections' are the key words there, my friend. And spreading what would be looked upon as potential rumors about a high-ranking DOD member involved in a terrorist attack—that would have put an end to my ability to get eyes inside of Aeneid."

"Sure this doesn't also have something to do with Israeli politics and their relations with Iran?"

Anatoly just gave him a sideways glance and grumbled. "I'm never one to back away from action that would cripple Iran's supreme leader, but not something that would compromise my government's relations with the U.S. in the process."

Mitch stared back at the laptop. "So where can you decode these files?"

Dev looked at him then at her father. She ran her hand through her thick mane of hair. "Aeneid is a sure bet. If we access their server, we can find out the details of what's about to unfold." She removed a small device from her shoulder bag and palmed it in her right hand. It was the size of a TV remote with a side port and two blinking red lights. The hi-tech gadget was something developed recently by Israeli intelligence and enabled the user to surreptitiously force pairing with another computer network within ten feet. It had allowed Dev to obtain the files days before at Aeneid and now she dreaded the thought of having to use it once more inside that wretched hive of lunatics.

"Surely they would've reconfigured their plans by now knowing you have this intel," said Mitch.

"The pipeline project in the Caspian Sea is slated to begin next week—seven days from today—so they're unlikely to have altered things on their end, especially since they thought Devorah would be out of the picture by now," said Anatoly, resting a hand on his daughter's shoulder.

Dev leaned back to stretch then looked at her watch. "If we're heading to Anaheim then we shouldn't delay."

"My thoughts exactly," said Anatoly, getting up. "I will talk with my men and go over the best routes there." He placed his empty glass on the table and suppressed a slight belch of pleasure from his elixir.

Dev looked at her laptop screen in frustration. "I never wanted to set foot inside Aeneid again. How did I miss this?"

"The thought that you even made it as far as you did there and got out is damn impressive," said Mitch. He realized just how close he was sitting next to her and he scooched back a few feet.

She glanced at his neckline and moved his shirt collar. "Ooh, looks like you've got some nasty scrapes there from all the bushwhacking we did."

He tucked in his chin, straining his eyes to the left to see. "It does feel like I was just in my first rodeo now that you mention it." He rolled his shoulders back, realizing how sore he was. She got up and walked over to the kitchen sink, returning with a damp washcloth.

She began dabbing the lacerations, pulling back his soiled collar slightly. "So you're a combat medic too, in addition to a spy and cyber-sleuth?" he said.

"Probably like you, I've had to become proficient at a lot of skills over being expert at one or two."

He looked at her, enjoying her touch but also wanting to pull away. "I didn't know Israeli women had such a caring side to them. At least not the ones I've worked with in the past."

"They don't but there are a few exceptional ones like me," she said with a grin while looking at his face. He returned the gaze, locking his eyes onto hers, then suddenly he grabbed the washcloth and stood up. "I'm good now, thanks. I...I appreciate the kind gesture."

Anatoly had re-entered, walking through the living room, and hesitated briefly when he saw the interaction. His slight smile faded as he informed them of their need to depart.

"The L.A. area is around six hundred miles from here. We will pick up another vehicle in Barstow. You and Dev will drive to the outskirts of Anaheim. My men and I will head to Aeneid near downtown."

"The outskirts—what for?" said Mitch.

"I'll explain as we head west. Sometimes the best solution is also the least obvious one."

27

FAREED MAHMOUD DROVE his black Honda Accord behind the rear of the shuttered two-story car stereo warehouse on Lampson Avenue, pausing long enough to see the moon flickering off the chipped cement walls. He had only been this far south in Anaheim a few times but he'd always carried a pistol which boosted his feeling of confidence in handling himself.

He'd trained overseas in the foothills in Yemen with a variety of weapons at an Al Qaeda affiliated camp but he'd never actually shot anyone and he longed for the coming attack when he could prove himself to Allah and his brethren. He watched any film that involved gun battles or warfare, studying the demeanor of the protagonist while mimicking the drawing and reholstering in front of the mirror in his shabby studio apartment adjacent to the university.

At last, the training, the prayers, the planning would all come to fruition in the next few days. His contact, Gamal, had proven trustworthy even for an Egyptian—Fareed had tailed him one night to confirm he was who he claimed. The other eight men in Fareed's inner circle were true believers like himself and would do what he commanded. They were younger but even more jaded than him. They had grown fond of hearing him recount his training days in Yemen, and their intensified drills in small-unit tactics during the past week had only strengthened their bonds.

He got out of the car, looking both ways, and then skulked up to the door, inserting the key to his uncle's old warehouse. Once inside, he walked around to the other exit doors and checked the egress routes outside to make sure they were clear just in case something went wrong during the upcoming exchange. Fareed then walked around the warehouse, picking up any debris left behind from their training activities and sweeping the assemblage of old boot prints dotting the dusty floor. He didn't want anything being connected to his uncle, who was a hard-working businessman, though he had been softened too much by his Western lifestyle.

When he was done grooming the place, he walked over to the windows by the large rolling garage door. He peered out beyond several rows of storage containers to an immense field that looked like a thatched blanket with its stalks of parched grass. Fareed looked up at the moon while extracting a bronze dagger from its leather sheath in his beltline. The blade had his family's crest stamped into the handle and it was one of his most treasured items, one that he felt spiritually connected him to his homeland.

He rolled up his left sleeve and looked at the seven parallel scars on his outer forearm. Each one a symbol of faith, to mark the months since he began this sacred undertaking. He slid the tip of the curved blade across his skin, making another two-inch-long incision, just deep enough to leave a future scar but not deep enough, like the first one, to require stitches. As the knife revealed its passage, he whispered up to the moon while clenching his teeth. "Without pain there is no reward in heaven." He repeated the words over and over and over as his blade hand shook and a rivulet of sweat rolled off his forehead. When the incision was complete, his frantic mantra stopped and his lips revealed a tremulous smile. He gasped from the exquisite pain which seemed almost euphoric in between the burning flares fired by his nerve endings.

He wrapped the wound with a roll of gauze from his jacket, making sure no blood droplets made it to the floor. He sucked down another deep breath and faced the moon, partly glancing at his own faint reflection in the window. Fareed put away his blade and then rested his palm on the pistol concealed in his waistline. He wished his will could move the earth to increase its revolutions so the next day would come sooner.

28

After leaving the cabin near Flagstaff, Anatoly discussed their plans for breaching Aeneid's security and gaining access to their computer network. His men had a duffle bag of weapons that Mitch and Dev resupplied from while hearing about Anatoly's scheme. Arriving at Barstow, California around three AM, Dev and Mitch were dropped off in a Motel Six parking lot. Dev had identified an older Subaru Forester parked under a burnt-out light that was worthy of procuring, much to Mitch's disapproving looks.

She stood beside the driver's door, working the entry with her small lockpicking set while Mitch scanned their surroundings for anyone up late enough to notice them.

"So I'm sure you thought about the family you're gonna leave stranded here when they get up in the morning," said Mitch. "You couldn't have chosen a more beat-up rig that maybe belonged to some dude passing through?"

"What's it matter? This vehicle is just another tool for getting the job done. They're insured and will have a new car by next week. Besides, I'm doing them a favor—did you see all the disgusting juice stains on the back seat?" She nodded to the rear while jimmying the door open.

"I just pity the poor bunch of folks that have to be stranded in Barstow."

She scrunched her nose at him and emitted a short grunt. "How you even have the time or mental energy to worry about such BS is beyond me. Tools are tools—weapons, vehicles, electronics, even people if necessary." She paused, looking at him for a second while contemplating the last word. "I didn't mean you, per se."

"Uh-huh. You owe my friend a new bunkhouse at his ranch, by the way." He exhaled, studying the parking lot near the rear of the hotel. "As for me, I haven't decided if I should thank you for yanking me out of a job I didn't really enjoy or if I should call my bureau chief again."

"Look, I'm sorry for the mess I brought upon you. It wasn't my intention. Life rarely goes according to one's wishes even when you have a well-thought-out plan, don't you agree?"

"I would agree that you operate in a world that is much grayer than mine. You seem bent on getting the job done regardless of how much mayhem it costs others around you."

She ignored his comment and started the vehicle, then hopped inside. "I'll drive first. You can entertain me with more of your tales of morality as we head west."

Mitch walked around and got in, stuffing the duffle bag with their rifles in the rear seat over the spilled Cheerios and empty Kool-Aid packets. Anatoly had provided them with additional ammunition, radios, flash-bang grenades, and suppressors for their pistols along with encrypted radios.

He admired Dev's spirit of pushing ahead regardless of how arduous the task but wondered if she really cared about anything other than reaching her end goal. He was already sucked in too deep to this plot to turn back and his innocence was riding on the completion of what lay ahead. Would she and Anatoly simply disappear afterwards, leaving him in their wake to put his career back together and face months of investigations from the Department of Justice? Or would he be stripped of his status as an agent, publicly disgraced, and then slapped with criminal fines? He didn't know but as he looked over at her while they zipped onto the entrance ramp, he was certain the coming day would be enlightening on many accounts and would be a far cry from the doldrums of his usual work.

For the next few hours while heading towards Anaheim, they discussed their upcoming roles, contingency plans, and fighting tactics if they came under fire. Mitch climbed into the back seat and did an inventory of the weapons along with tearing through a beef stroganoff MRE packet that Anatoly had provided.

"I feel sorry for you soldiers in the American military who have to live on that kind of *food* when you're deployed."

"Yeah, Meals-Refused-by-Ethiopians is what we call it. Hell, I once had to do sixty-seven days on this shit during a long mission. They'd do helo resupply drops once a week. You know things are bad when you start having dreams about a juicy steak that knows your name."

"That's another difference between our two countries' militaries—we believe long-term care of the body is as essential as the mind, given how many decades we have been in continuous conflict. We openly acknowledge the reality of PTSD and don't consider it a stigma on our record if we seek treatment."

She glanced at him in the rearview mirror. "America has

long been our ally but your country is used to coming and going from different theaters of operation depending on the administration at the time. My people have had a war on their doorstep since my grandmother's childhood. When you go to sleep at night in your bedroom to the thunder of distant mortar fire, you grow up knowing that the world is a fractured place."

Mitch thought of his own youth on his uncle's ranch, which had become a sanctuary for him after his parents' untimely deaths. The honest work with his hands out on the land gave him a sense of purpose and helped to heal his spirit. Having known firsthand the effects that constant combat in war-torn regions has upon the psyche, he couldn't imagine what Dev's childhood was like growing up amidst the daily threat of terrorism. It explained the raw edge she had at times and Mitch wondered if her mother was the sole reason the woman still had a glimmer of trust in her eyes. Surely Anatoly would have, consciously or otherwise, imparted another set of traits altogether.

Mitch saw the green sign for downtown Anaheim emerge on the interstate overpass. The sooner they got this done the better. Not only did he desperately need to find out what was on that file but he despised being in large cities. Even Phoenix made him claustrophobic and edgy.

They did a verbal rundown of their roles one more time as Dev drove past the freeway exit that led to Aeneid, continuing west.

"How did you get hired on and insert yourself there?"

"Once Aeneid's involvement in the Caspian Sea region was identified through the hostage we rescued, I spent the next seven months slowly building a relationship with their cyber security director, Jessica Carter." She could see Mitch's eyes widen in the mirror. "No, not that kind of relationship."

She changed lanes and continued the story. "I established rapport with her at several insider trade conventions open to DOD contractors, eventually gaining her trust and convincing her that I knew the field. This was not hard to do given my background in cyber security but my father's organization also played a role in forging the false identity of Mira Sanchez."

"Is that how you've managed to stay out of the databases for so long? You never showed up when I was searching for Anatoly."

"Precisely, although he started with me at an early age, making sure I had no digital presence online or later on social media sites. He knew back in the '90s what was coming with the cyber world and our personal security. You won't find anything on me except a few photos he's planted and even those have cosmetic changes from the real me."

"'The real you'—when do I get to see that person or is this her?"

"She's crept out a few times. Maybe you should pay more attention." She gave him a coy smile in the mirror and then pointed to their exit. "Twenty minutes and we'll be at our destination."

29

Perry was standing amidst numerous security monitors in the control room on the ground floor of the Aeneid Corporation. On the brief flight from Phoenix to Anaheim on Ritter's company jet, Perry had changed into his usual suit and dress slacks, his two Sig P229 pistols riding on shoulder holsters.

The double doors swung over and Aeneid's new security chief walked in, having recently received his promotion after Drake's demise. He moved alongside Perry, who was still busy staring at the monitors.

"My name's Seth Garretson, head of security. Mr. Ritter informed me of your arrival."

Perry gave him a sideways glance, his forehead creasing. "Seth—that sounds like the name of a fucking banker. You ever done mop-up operations like this before?"

Seth rolled his shoulders back, a smug grin issuing forth from his lips. "More than a few times in several countries."

"Good, 'cause I want you to impress the shit out of me by doing exactly what I tell you to—got it?" he said, inching closer to Seth, who took a slight step back.

Seth looked over his shoulder, pointing to the monitors. "We've got cameras on every entrance in the lobby, sub-basement, and exit doors of the entire building as well as in each elevator. If someone tries to breach the place, we'll see it."

"What about the terminals where files can be opened?"

Seth tapped his finger on a gray monitor to the far left. "Only one place in the entire facility—the mainframe on the fifth floor. It has three levels of security doors and the guards have been doubled. All of the entrances have been sealed except in the front lobby. The stairwells, rooftop, and fire escapes are all locked up tighter than a camel's ass in a sandstorm."

Perry placed his hands on his hips. "How many men do you have at your disposal?"

"Eighteen ex-military with extensive experience and then a dozen more of our regular security guards who will go where they're needed."

Perry ran through all the figures in his head and then studied the black-and-white images on the screens before him. *Good thing Mitch is a fucking redneck. He'll be out of his element in the city. That woman is the wild card though. She's probably tugging him along for the ride, giving his pathetic life some sense of purpose. She's the one who could slip by if we missed something.*

Ritter walked in and moved between the two men, causing Seth's facial muscles to quiver as he stepped aside.

"Has my man provided everything you need?" said Ritter, running his tongue over his capped teeth.

"He did and he's not half the Neanderthal that Drake was so we should be good. Now we just have to sit tight and wait, assuming they come."

Ritter folded his arms and glanced at Perry. "Trust me,

they'll be here. It's the only way for them to read what's on that file and to clear their names. Without that, they know they'll be on the run for good."

Ritter moved away and stepped into a side room to call Monroe on his cellphone. "My good man, in another two hours you will be richer than God."

"So, it's underway," the assistant sec-def replied while making a chewing sound.

"Soon; the shipment has arrived and will be dispersed to the main players. Tomorrow at this time all eyes will be upon Iran and they will be forced to pull out of the disputed pipeline boundaries."

"And here I thought I was having a good day with this Argentinian filet mignon on my plate. What about making sure there's no trace back to you, my friend?"

"Aeneid will soon be clear of any worries," he said, looking through the door window at the security monitors. "Plus, the target is a college campus that my daughter from my third marriage attends, which will further place me out of the spotlight. Not to worry, though, she's supposed to be away in Spain this week."

"After all of this is over, we must get together again in Tahoe and hash out the details of the mergers for the pipeline and accompanying villages that will need to be removed."

"I'll be in touch shortly."

Ritter put his phone away and looked out the window again, this time studying Perry. *What to do with him after this is over? Maybe I should hire him on directly for overseeing the project abroad. He could be a further asset and obtaining another fed that's even slightly competent is such a headache.*

Perry resembled so many other ladder-climbing miscreants who could be wound up for hire with the proper six-figure inducement. That's why Ritter lamented Drake's demise. He was a simple brute who was good at squashing problems and had few aspirations in life other than serving at the feet of a good master who patted him on the head every few months. *Still, Perry could work given the proper incentives.* Ritter emitted a bleak smile, his face looking like old parchment in the fluorescent lighting while he mulled over the power he was about to hold in his palm and what he would do with the life of the man in the next room.

30

KETAMINE WAS a tricky drug to use on humans. Too much and the subject wouldn't recover, succumbing to heart failure. Too little and you'd have a wobbly drunk coherent enough to trigger the alarm and foil your breaching plans.

The use of ketamine by covert operatives was considered old school and many of the newer operators simply relied on more powerful opiates that were less risky. Anatoly however had used the drug enough to be able to roughly estimate the subject's weight to deliver the approximate dosage. More importantly, the drug and accompanying rifle could be obtained through surreptitious entry into a veterinary clinic, which Anatoly had done on 7th and Broadway in a quick after-hours stop he and his men had made in Bakersfield. The rifle was used for subduing feral dogs or the occasional coyote or bobcat that wandered into the neighborhood and Anatoly had liberated it from the clinic along with a number of other sedatives.

As he squatted on one knee in the bushes beside the electric fence of the building ahead, he slipped the miniscule dart inside the tranquilizer rifle and steadied the front sight on the lone guard, twenty yards distant. Killing wasn't in the plan for breaching the compound unless things really went south, though he wouldn't hesitate to drive a round through Nelson Ritter's caveman skull if given the opportunity tonight.

He had never met the man but all of his covert work during the years kept pointing to the despicable creature as the conductor of endless suffering in the nations bordering the Caspian Sea. Thwarting his plans would put an end to the strife Ritter had promulgated for decades, costing the lives of thousands of innocent villagers in Turkmenistan where the proposed oil pipeline was supposed to be constructed.

Anatoly's mind drifted back to another time and what seemed like a different era of warfare. Just after the fall of the Soviet Union in 1991, Turkmenistan went from being a Soviet constituent to its sovereign nation. Many other countries, including Israel, wanted to have their claws sunk into the back of the world's fourth largest reserve of natural gas. Anatoly was a young Mossad officer on his first major assignment overseas. His unit inserted into the Badkyz desert region that bordered northeastern Iran and provided training and support for Turkmen rebels fighting against a newly formed group called Al Qaeda that had just recently sprung up along the border in northwestern Afghanistan. The Cold War carryover of the mujahedeen were hoping to gain a foothold for opium production fields in the newly formed country of Turkmenistan.

Anatoly was instructed to teach the ad-hoc group of Turkmen rebels that were strung out in villages over a hundred mile region in the Sangar Valley, a rugged desert region that depended on a centuries-old trade route to move cotton to ports in the Caspian Sea. For eight months, he lived and trained with the hardy desert dwellers whose austere lifestyle he came to admire, eventually growing fond of a young widow and her son.

During the onset of fall, he was to lead their first large resistance fight against a fledgling Al Qaeda group massing near the mountain pass thirty miles to the southwest. Policy intervened at the last minute, the order to pull out coming from central command in Israel. He later found out this was caused by dwindling support for the rebellion in U.S. political circles due to their backing of the Gulf War, which had just unfolded. Anatoly and his men along with their battery of weapon platforms situated in the mountains were recalled within days.

Two weeks after returning to Tel Aviv, he learned that the main villages in the Sangar Valley were overrun by armored vehicles from Afghanistan, his informants and friends amongst the Turkmen either dead or missing. Eventually news of the deaths of the young woman and her little boy reached him. He still remembered the dreadful December day that tore the fabric of his soul. Anatoly never spoke of the failed mission and its aftermath except to his daughter and only then after the veil of secrecy was removed by the Israeli government when they de-listed classified documents years later.

He had spent the past thirty years doing what he could to trickle his own funds to the few survivors in Sangar, trying to rebuild their villages. With the formation of his own company, he opened several relief charities for people in Turkmenistan and always looked for ways to insert his organization into rescue operations there.

Now with the impending pipeline that Ritter was planning to build, the Sangar Valley people would be forcibly relocated or even eradicated if Ritter could find a way.

Anatoly took a deep breath and focused his mind back in the present, inhaling the fragrance of the lilacs around him. He looked over at Petra, who was disabling the electric fence at the junction box a hundred yards to his right. The young man with the anemic goatee turned and gave him a thumbs-up. Anatoly refocused his rifle sight and sent the projectile downrange into the soft tissue above the guard's clavicle. The man winced, staggered a few feet to the entrance door, and collapsed on the blacktop.

Petra and three other men began feverishly snipping a small entrance through the fence with their bolt cutters while Anatoly kept his eyes focused on the building entrance and main road. Thirty seconds later, they all crawled through, running in a low squat across the open field to the steel front door. Anatoly paused to check the guard's pulse while Petra took the man's keys and opened the heavy door.

The sign above them indicated, *State of California Power Relay Substation #12.*

The location was ideal: off the main roads, minimally protected, and of small significance to the larger power grid in California. Anatoly's computer techs back in Israel had identified the sight for its vestigial connection to estates and businesses located in northwest Anaheim. Aeneid's internal power systems were too well-protected to breach from inside and they had their own internal generator system in the event of any issues with the power grid.

However, any ripple effect in the electricity output from the relay substation would send an immediate alert to the Los Angeles County Fire Department which would then dispatch units to each of the affected homes or businesses to inquire about critical power surges that could result in fires. Such lessons were gleaned from the '94 Northridge earthquake and it was standard protocol for electrical-related emergencies.

Anatoly walked to the back room, opening the door silently and slipping behind another guard at a work station. He artfully slid his arms around the man's wispy neck, employing a sleeper hold, then lowered his limp figure to the floor. He stood before the control console, searching for the manual override lever that would temporarily deactivate the current emanating from the forty acres of electrical towers outside the building.

He found the lever and then glanced at his watch. "Four minutes," he muttered to his men behind him who were fanned out along the entrance door. "That's a long time to be stuck in a building with only one exit."

31

Mitch was kneeling beside a terraced assemblage of rocks near the entrance to a two-story mansion. The eight-foot-high wrought-iron fence came to a flared point sharp enough to deter a climber. He knew it was also electrified given the faint humming emanating from the main support posts.

Through his binoculars he could make out the shapes of two Rottweilers roaming around the front entrance. The manicured lawn between the fence and the house was nearly one hundred feet long and he knew that such trained dogs would be on him within seconds. Mitch had done extensive counter-dog training against Belgian Malinois attack dogs while in the Special Forces and was well aware of the savagery contained beneath their stolid eyes.

"Why the hell didn't we get a tranq gun like your pops?" he whispered to Dev, who knelt a few feet away, her eyes fixed on her small laptop screen.

Dev sighed and hit her fist against her leg. "We have to get closer to the house. I can't force my computer to pair with Nelson's system from here."

Mitch rubbed the whiskers on his chin and took a hard swallow as he looked at the Rotties again. "What the hell do you mean, 'pairing it from here'? I thought we were going inside to use his setup to decrypt the file you have."

"The computer network inside Ritter's estate is routed into the mainframe at Aeneid, true, but it doesn't access critical files like the one in my possession. However, if I can hack into his remote work terminal from here and route it through Jessica Carter's system in her office, we should be able to access it that way. Coupled with the power blackout my father is about to implement, it will hopefully create the panic needed at Aeneid to drive them to their weapons cache."

Mitch grabbed her arm, pivoting her slightly. "You can't access the files you have at all, can you? You never could."

"At first I suspected it might work but the more I labored on it last night at the cabin, the more I realized the encryption was unbreakable except at Aeneid. If we can draw them out, make them think we've gained access through Carter's system, then they can lead us to the staging area."

"When were you going to tell me this?"

"Only when I knew for sure it was our only option. My father said you can be, well," she paused, weighing her words, "rigid when it comes to certain things." She averted her eyes from his and resumed glancing at her laptop. "I was here once for a work party he and his wife put on so I know the general layout. I need to be within twenty feet of the house for my malware to slip past the cyber defenses in his home office."

Mitch kept glaring at her while shaking his head. "You and your old man make a good pair alright—all these endless fucking secrets. You sure that's the world you want to live in?" He shrugged his shoulders and exhaled. "Anything else I should know?"

"Yeah, I need to be within twenty goddam feet of Ritter's house—you got that?!"

He muttered to himself and then stood in a partial squat, waving his arm furiously for her to follow him along the fence line to the rear of the property.

"What's your plan for tracking them if they buy into this?"

"I've got satellite imagery of their facility and my computer is set up for auto-surveillance of any of their vehicles coming or going from Aeneid."

"Ah, I don't even want to know what satellite was hacked to obtain that."

"I wasn't going to tell you anyway, cowboy."

Arriving at the rear of the property, Mitch reached into his pack and carefully removed six water balloons whose liquid contents were an amalgamation of bacon bits, sardines, and peanut butter that he had picked up at a grocery store on the outskirts of Anaheim. "If this concoction doesn't work, then I don't know what will." He readied one of the balloons in his palm. "Most high-end guard dogs won't defer to a slab of meat laced with tranquilizers tossed on the ground as they've been forcibly trained out of that temptation. This shit, though, will trigger their scent drive long enough to distract them while you work your magic."

She looked at the flash-bang grenades dangling off his vest. "You can always go the easy route. It won't kill them."

"No, but it will fuck their hearing up for life. Ritter is the only one that's a true son of a bitch, not the dogs."

Dev glanced at her watch, counting down the seconds to the timeline she and her father had calibrated on their watches. It was nearly 4 AM and they would lose the benefit of darkness soon. She raised her hand up, showing her five fingers extended, then counted down as the designated time arrived. When the last finger folded, Mitch flung the balloons thirty feet onto the pavement by the nearest wall then whistled. The exterior security lights went dim as Anatoly's sabotage efforts came to fruition.

Dev bolted a hundred yards down to the gate and belly-crawled under the tiny spacing, making sure not to touch the metal in case the power went back on unexpectedly. Confirming that the dogs were gone, she ran from shrub to shrub until she was at the back wall. With her laptop bag slung on her back, she climbed up the protruding exterior rock façade until she reached a patio on the second floor. She saw French doors with thick glass. Inside was Ritter's office with the computer a few feet away.

Dev knew the type of security system Ritter had in place and that she had to use her laptop malware to force pairing with his computer before the main power came back online. Once a modern hard drive was affected by power loss, its older network systems were vulnerable for a few minutes until security patches were overlaid. Dev began typing, uploading the malware that would insert itself into a back door into Aeneid's mainframe via the portal inside the office. Whether she could access the file in her possession was another story but it would alert the technicians at Aeneid that there was a security breach and hopefully put the dice in play.

She just wanted this to be over. Too much time away from home, away from her parents, and submerging herself as Mira Sanchez had chipped away the layers of her psyche. She wasn't sure if she was cut out to take over her father's company one day as he had alluded to and while she was good at what she did, the main reason for staying was to be closer to him. *Hopefully this will do it and my life can return to some version of normal. How I miss Tel Aviv, my mother's cooking, and the smell of cedars.* She saw the icon for the file indicating it was opening. Dev hastily scanned the documents and email headings, searching for the answers she had so desperately sought for days.

Down below, Mitch kept his suppressed pistol focused on the Rottweilers, which had swung over his way after the shrill sound only to come to a temporary halt at the wall of scent hovering over the cement pathway. The strong odor in the air was almost too much for him and he kept holding his breath.

A few minutes later, he saw Dev climbing down from the upstairs porch. A moment later, the lights flickered back on, illuminating her in the open like a dancer in the spotlight. The Rottweilers immediately caught sight of her movement and emitted a low growl, which turned into machine-gun barking before they bounded off in her direction.

There was no time to use the flash-bangs and it would only impair Dev's escape. He took off running along the fence, raising his pistol and firing off two rounds into a propane tank attached to the outdoor barbecue. The patio erupted in a small mushroom cloud, rattling the back windows and sending lawn chairs airborne. The dogs split apart in a panic, veering off from their trajectory and away from their target. They retreated to either side of a woodshed at the property's edge while Dev retraced her steps under the fence, making it to the curb where Mitch caught up with her.

"Nicely done," he said. "Now all we need is a helicopter

to whisk us away to the crime scene I hope you're gonna tell me you got the location of."

She gave him a thumbs-up as they sprinted back to their vehicle. "Everything but the helo, anyway."

Getting inside, Mitch gunned the Subaru down the winding road to the city lights below.

32

Ryker was sitting at his desk at the downtown Phoenix office, tapping his pencil rhythmically on his laptop screen while analyzing the recent information from Interpol that had just arrived. The image of a woman who went by a half-dozen aliases pulled up. Ryker's pencil stopped fluttering as he sat upright in his chair then hastily tore through papers on his desk, searching for the FBI bulletin he'd received the day before. He held the photograph of Mira Sanchez next to the new one, his eyes narrowing. Beside the listed aliases were the words: *Person of Interest in international espionage undertakings and cyber-hacking.*

Ryker picked up the phone and dialed Perry's number, going straight to voicemail. He mentally replayed the details of the previous day's debriefing with Perry and then reflected on Mitch's disturbing phone call, which contradicted everything he'd been told. Ryker leaned back in his chair, folding his arms while staring at the original FBI bulletin. He picked it up again, studying the image and text. *How did this woman make it up on the list so quickly without all the usual bureaucratic red tape?*

Ryker picked up the phone and dialed in the tech and ballistics division on the second floor. "I'd like to put a trace on Agent Perry Kovac's phone. Notify me when you have his location."

He put the phone down and stood up, balling his fists and pressing them into the edge of his desk, staring pensively at his laptop as he waited for the information to arrive. Ryker wasn't sure who to believe but something didn't feel right about Perry's earlier dismissal of Mitch and the botched field operation that had unfolded in the desert. He was also surprised at how quickly the facial recognition software request had been approved by the D.C. office. That hadn't ever happened in his twelve years on the job.

The phone rang, the call coming from the technician he'd just spoken with. "Sir, I've got his location and I'm sending it over right now but you might also be interested to know that the ballistics report on our three agents came in—the rounds were identical to the hollow point rounds found in the dead men's weapons at the ranch house. They are proprietary rounds that come out of Latin America. There's no way Agent Kearns could have fired those shots."

He saw the map pop up on his laptop with a concentric circle pulsing around the city of Anaheim, California. He thanked the technician and enhanced the imagery on his screen, after which GPS coordinates pulled up. He clicked on the numbers. Ryker's eyes went wide as he stood back. "Aeneid Corporation."

Ryker grabbed his jacket and his tactical gear bag then phoned the operations center to scramble the helicopter on the roof.

33

Perry's earpiece crackled as the guard in the lobby notified him of four firefighters who had arrived, requesting to get verification that their electrical power supply was unaffected by the recent rolling blackout. He scanned the security monitors, searching for any signs of Mitch or Sanchez, but saw nothing. *They're probably trying to use the firefighters for cover—or are concealed as one of the firefighters.*

He spun around and trotted to the door. "On my way down. Keep the fire crew there."

Ritter stopped him, pressing his hand into the door. "Are you insane? You can't be seen here. You're a federal agent who's supposed to be in Arizona right now."

Perry arched his shoulders back, wanting to drive his fist into the old man's face but knowing he was right. He yelled back to the security chief Seth. "Get over to the lobby and make sure those guys check out. Then do a sweep of the computer mainframe again to make sure everything is secure."

Perry swept back to the console, staring squarely at the firemen, trying to enhance the resolution of their faces. One of them had his back to the camera and hadn't moved since their arrival. "Dammit, that has to be Mitch." He slammed his fist against the desk, his eyes scouring every nuance of the man's features as Seth entered the frame. A minute later, Perry received confirmation in his earpiece that the men checked out and he saw that the fireman was not whom he suspected. He blinked his eyes hard, trying to relax, then saw Seth escort the men towards the circuit breaker room at the back of the lobby. Perry took several deep breaths, trying to calm his mind, knowing his imagination was starting to erode his normally calm mindset.

Perry had to fight back his acid reflux, which was getting out of control. His mind was racing over the variables that seemed to be unspooling around him. This was supposed to be a quick operation to nab the woman. Then he could melt back into his role at the FBI so he wouldn't be missed in Phoenix. Ritter had layers of deniability to cover his ass but Perry was starting to feel a chill coming over his own. Something needed to happen fast. All he felt like doing was putting his fist through someone's face but instead he ground his teeth and seethed, resuming his search for intruders on the monitors ahead.

Lawry, the systems engineer sitting to Perry's right, began tapping on a blinking red light on the console.

"What—what's wrong? What the hell is that?" said Perry.

"Not sure, but someone is trying to gain access to our systems." The bald man began typing on his keyboard, pulling up different screens that showed the internal schematics of the facility. He checked the mainframe on the fifth floor which indicated the vault door was still secure. Then he wheeled his chair over to another monitor to search the security system on Jessica Carter's old office. "I don't get it, the main terminal is secure but it appears that there is an attempted breach through the portals in Carter's office."

Perry grabbed the man's shirt collar, scrunching the fabric enough to put a choke on his throat. "This is the part where you get a chiropractic adjustment if I don't get fucking results in the next minute."

Lawry began frantically typing, reducing the signal down to the source until the schematic of the facility pulled up again. This time a red line emanating from Aeneid began etching itself along the screen, leading across the city.

"What is that? Some remote terminal?" yelled Perry. "Do they have access?"

"I'll know in just a moment."

Perry raced to the back of the room beside the other office and yanked open the door where Ritter was located. "I'm pretty sure we're fucked—they may have found a way in."

The two men rushed back to the console where Lawry had just finished his last keyboard stroke. The red line simulating the source ended in a residential area where it kept pulsing. "They must have a mobile site outside the city," said Perry.

Ritter's mouth hung open and the color had drained out of his normally tan face. "No...no, that's my estate."

Perry grabbed Nelson's arm. "Is your terminal there secure or are they waltzing through your fucking firewall upstairs right now?"

Ritter paused, his lips trembling and his fists balling up. "They shouldn't be able to breach our system."

"*Shouldn't be able to*—Christ. We need to get the shipment moved and in the hands of Fareed and his guys so we're clear of this." Perry unhanded the older man and staggered to the door. "Don't tell me about going out in public now. You've given me little choice."

Ritter followed behind him. "I'm coming as well. Besides, you don't even know the location and will need reinforcements if this thing goes to hell."

34

Within minutes of receiving the alert at Aeneid, Ritter and Perry sped out of the facility, racing towards the warehouse where the weapons shipment was about to be delivered. Ritter alerted his team of henchmen that were already on site to be on the lookout for anything out of the ordinary and to hasten the arms exchange with Fareed.

Dev was watching the satellite feed on her computer from the comfort of their stolen van when the visual she'd hoped for emerged. "Looks like the fox has fled the henhouse. I've got 'em." Mitch was in the driver's seat peeling along the interstate. Nearing the warehouse location, Mitch grabbed the cellphone out of Dev's shoulder bag and called Ryker.

"I have the proof. Perry is moving a shipment of assault weapons and IED materials through Aeneid to a group of Iranian terrorists. Thomas Monroe is in on it too."

"Assistant Secretary of Defense Monroe?"

"Exactly. Perry is the liaison between the two. He's been

using bureau resources to cover their tracks. It all unfolds tonight at the warehouse on Lamson and Brookhurst in Anaheim."

"It should interest you to know that I've just uncovered some disturbing details about Perry's involvement in this whole thing. Ballistics also confirmed that you weren't the shooter, as I suspected all along."

Mitch took a deep breath and relaxed his clenched fist.

"Listen, Mitch, whatever this is about, this lady Mira Sanchez is knee-deep in it. She came up on an Interpol search and has a pretty shocking rap sheet and numerous aliases. In fact, I'm not even sure which one, if any, is her real name. If she's with you then you may have more than Perry and Aeneid to worry about."

He looked over at Dev, who was giving him a quizzical look. "Yeah, I can only imagine. Good thing we parted ways a while back. She seemed like too much of a loose cannon anyway."

35

FAREED and his eight fellow jihadists were waiting in the rear of the warehouse, fanned out around their two cars when two black Ford F-150s rolled into the parking lot outside. He motioned for the other men to stay put while he ran to the dusty bay windows, withdrawing his pistol from the Kydex holster on his belt. Fareed saw two men with beards and long jackets emerge, one of them being Gamal, the contact that he'd set up the weapons exchange with. Despite his attempt to steady his breathing, his limbs still pulsed with adrenaline, causing his entire body to feel like he had harnessed the power of the sun. His head filled with images of tomorrow's news when his face would be heralded across the world for his exploits.

"It's OK, my brothers," he said to the others at his rear. "Open the garage and let them in."

A stout man walked to the side of the building near the truck and hoisted up the large folding door. Fareed came up alongside him and waved the driver in.

As the truck started to move, Fareed caught sight of

headlights in the distance, the intensity increasing with each second. "What is this—a trick, you bastard?" he yelled at Gamal through his open window.

"Relax, my man. That's just my boss wanting to make sure everything goes off according to the plan."

When the gray SUV pulled up, a man stepped briskly out of the passenger's side. He was dressed in a suit and resembled what Fareed imagined an undercover cop would look like. There was an older man sitting in the back seat, staring intently through the tinted window, his gaunt face barely visible in the dim lighting. Three other rough-looking fellows also moved around to the front, their hands resting in front of the openings in their jackets.

"Let's get this shipment unloaded now," snapped the well-dressed man at Gamal, then gave a fierce look to Fareed. "Have your men pull their vehicles up so we can get these items dispersed and you can be on your way."

Ten minutes later, with their vehicles nearly full of the payload, Fareed cracked open one of the crates to inspect the treasure trove of weapons. His eyes danced along the contours of the dozen AK-47s. They were identical to the type he had trained with in Yemen months ago, only these had receivers that had been stamped with the Iranian flag. He slid a rifle out and was about to ask the man in the suit about this when he saw another set of headlights racing towards them. This vehicle was not slowing down.

"Get the hell out of here," yelled the man in the suit as he sprinted for the SUV but then veered off behind some crates as the approaching Subaru slammed into the rear of the gray vehicle, sending it towards Fareed.

He tossed the empty AK on the ground and leapt onto the pavement, coming up in an awkward somersault. The lead vehicle was sending rivulets of gasoline along the ground and the air filled with vapors. Fareed saw two people emerge from the van. One was a scruffy man who ran in the direction of the crates while the other was a lean woman who moved like a jaguar and was heading straight for him.

36

Dev had the young would-be terrorist in her sights as she sprinted from the vehicle and charged him. Gamal darted out in a linebacker's tackle to intercept her, only to have her sidestep at the last second and clothesline him under the chin with her forearm. The big Egyptian's feet went skyward and he landed on his back. She lunged at him, driving her heel into his groin then kicking forward into his chin.

With the burly thug out of the way, she continued running past the damaged SUV where she caught sight of Ritter inside, his head leaking blood while the driver appeared to have a contorted neck. A half-dozen middle-eastern men were spreading out like oil droplets on a hot skillet as they began wildly shooting at Ritter's henchmen in the parking lot.

Dev swung around the back of a car whose trunk was loaded with weapons crates and came at Fareed with a running jump kick to his chest. He toppled backwards into a pile of pallets, springing back up on his feet, his pistol lying on the ground after becoming dislodged from its cheap holster. Fareed reached behind his back, pulling out his nine-inch bronze dagger. He brandished the blade in a reverse-grip fashion, keeping it close to his side.

Dev removed her own blade, a six-inch folder, and whipped it open. If possible, she wanted the man alive so she could get information regarding the attack. Fareed lunged forward, his blade hand delivering a short slash at her forearm. She deftly sidestepped, slicing at his triceps, cutting deep into the muscle. The man winced and yelled at her in Persian, switching the knife to his other hand.

"You can surrender now or I will shred you one limb at a time until you've stopped, but I need one of you alive," she said, holding her dripping weapon at waist height in a move that intentionally invited him to attack. She had used the technique many times before to disarm an attacker she needed alive.

Fareed's breathing was furious, his facial muscles spasming from the pain in his arm. He glanced around at the mayhem unfolding around him and at the open trunk where the dormant weapons lay. Then he clutched his blade and focused his gaze upon Dev. "No fucking woman talks to me like that, you American whore."

"Wrong on both accounts," she said, arcing away from his incoming thrust and gashing him across the rear deltoid. His blade dropped and he fell on one knee. Dev saw that Petra had already subdued one of Fareed's men near the entrance door. She had diverted her attention for a microsecond too long, which allowed Fareed to drive his shin across the back of her calf, sweeping her foot out from under her.

Dev fell hard on her back as the adrenaline-crazed man sprung on top of her. She blocked his volley of punches then drove the pommel of her blade into his floating ribs until they snapped. As Fareed recoiled, she reversed the grip and drove the knife into his heart, hearing the blade break on a section of sternum, then shoved him back onto the pavement. Quickly bolting to her feet, she went over to the writhing figure whose lips flowed with arterial blood.

"I should've done this to begin with," she said.

Dev felt the back of her right arm sear with pain as a pistol round grazed her skin. Instinctively she pivoted and ran for cover towards Fareed's car as more rounds zinged past her head from Ritter's gun. The old man had turned his weapon towards one of Fareed's men, shooting the heavily bearded figure in the head beside the garage door.

Dev removed her Glock and returned fire, sending Ritter for cover towards the corner of the building. A second later, there was automatic weapons fire emanating from outside—Anatoly had arrived with his men, all of them doing bounding moves along the parking lot while engaging the rest of Fareed's guys and Ritter's henchmen, who were fanned out around the vehicles. She saw Ritter fire at Anatoly, who staggered slightly and then returned the favor, driving the silver-haired man back into the alley.

Dev focused her vision and her fury on Ritter. He couldn't snake his way out of here and disappear. He had to be made accountable for this atrocious plot and have his involvement publicly exposed to bring down Aeneid. Seeing his shadow creep across the windows outside the rear entrance, she bolted across the warehouse to intercept him. Above the cacophony of gunfire, she heard the wail of sirens in the distance and knew the FBI would soon change the scope of what she could do, not to mention preventing her and her father's team from getting away undetected.

Dev ran for the exit door, scooping up Fareed's bronze dagger and tucking it inside her leather belt. Leaving the building, she saw Ritter sprinting past a gauntlet of empty wood crates as he sped along the alley. She did a fifty-yard dash and then came to an abrupt halt, focusing her sights on his right calf. The round she fired tore through enough of his flesh to cause him to careen to the side into a cluster of metal drums.

When she arrived at his side, Ritter was trying to slither towards his fallen pistol while shrieking. She kicked it away and grabbed his silver hair, yanking his head up. How she wanted to keep pulling until the vertebrae separated and his life slipped away. She flipped him over instead, looking into his tan face. "It's over. You, Monroe, Aeneid, it's all over."

She thought she heard him mutter something but it was drowned out by the sound of Petra's voice coming from her rear. She moved up beyond Ritter so she could keep him in sight and turned towards her colleague. Petra was heading her way with Anatoly clinging to his shoulders, a blood stain covering the center of her father's chest underneath his leather jacket. She felt her insides coil up and her breathing constrict. His face was pale and he was wheezing as the two men staggered up to her.

She glanced down at Ritter, whose grimace had turned to a grin. Then she knelt down and viciously smacked her pistol barrel against his forehead, knocking him out.

Dev turned back to embrace Anatoly. "Poppa," she whispered, using a name she hadn't uttered since she was a little girl. He fell into her arms and she lowered him to the ground, Petra moving off a few feet to stand guard with his MP-5. Dev looked at the gaping wound and into her father's diminishing eyes, feeling her own heart fibers shredding.

"No, Poppa—you mustn't leave now. Not now. We've made it so far together. You can't leave me now."

Anatoly reached his hand up, brushing a lock of brunette hair off her cheek as tears began streaming down his own. "You are what is best in my life—always remember that. I only wish I could have been there for you more, my beautiful daughter."

She clutched his sagging body to her chest, her arms trembling. "You're here now. You're here with me, right now—we have so much to do in this life. So much time to be together."

He forced out a bronchial cough, his breathing growing shallow. "The people of the Sangar Valley will need your help. Promise me you'll look after them, for I could not, not like I should have."

Dev gave him a reassuring nod, her tears streaming uncontrollably and her chest heaving as Anatoly slumped into her side, his eyes closing with his last exhale.

Their white van pulled up at the rear of the alley and one of Anatoly's men hopped out, looking at the fallen warrior with great sorrow etched on his face. "We have to go, the feds are almost here."

Dev shouted up to the sky, her tormented yelling blocking out the shriek of sirens in the distance. "No! He can't leave," she yelled up in Petra's face as he reached down to help her. The two men slowly lifted Anatoly and arranged his body in the van while Dev remained frozen to the pavement. She ran up to Ritter, kicking his limp figure in the ribs before Petra grabbed her in a bear-hug from behind and ushered her over to the van.

37

When the fighting broke out at the warehouse, Mitch saw Perry bolt for cover to the right of the building, disappearing behind three rows of red shipping containers that stretched for a half-mile along a grassy field. To the far right was a large cement wall that ran perpendicular to the highway. Running in a crouched position, Mitch rounded the corner of the first metal container and scanned the escape routes ahead.

He had noticed earlier that Perry was dressed in his usual FBI attire, including his black Converse dress shoes. Though Mitch wouldn't be able to discern any tread patterns in the gray pea-gravel between the containers, he saw the faint dishing pattern associated with someone sprinting, the stride increase and blown-out substrate revealing itself to his trained eyes. The tables had turned and now Perry was on the run, only this time there would be no canyons or mesas to disappear into. Mitch had tracked fugitives through urban areas before and knew it involved as much knowledge about human psychology as it did about locating visual clues.

With the sound of gunfire behind him, he slid between the first rows of containers for protection and then scanned the region ahead. The grassy field would be too exposed for Perry to risk fleeing in that direction and he wouldn't want to get pinned inside the abandoned warehouses lining the street to the left. The route ahead was the best option for evasion. *If he sprinted in and out of the containers until he reached the edge of the parking lot a half-mile in the distance, Perry would most likely use the concrete wall to the right for cover while fleeing east back to the city.*

Mitch kept his Glock at a low-ready as he maneuvered through the narrow path between shipping containers, following the displaced gravel impressions to stay on the trail. At each juncture between rows, he would have to pause and clear the route ahead. This was burning up too much time and he worried that it would increase Perry's chance of getting away. He stopped to take a breath, the rattle of gunfire to his rear growing faint.

Mitch was going to have to risk what Perry would not and make a dash across the open meadow. It was a gamble he had to take to intersect Perry's direction of travel behind the concrete wall. If the timing went smoothly, the wall would block Perry's view of the field long enough for Mitch to beat him to the highway. Mitch craned his head out from between the last row of containers, their red hue reflecting off the tawny blades of dry grass like the tail feathers of a giant macaw.

Damn, this is going to be a shooting gallery without any cover if he sees me. He took a deep breath, convincing himself again that this was the best route, then he darted into the meadow. Mitch's boots crunched over the dry stalks, his head twisting to the left, looking for any signs of Perry poking up from the wall to snipe him. His heart raced faster than usual and he wasn't sure if it was from the frantic pace or from the fear of being so exposed. He didn't bother zig-zagging to make himself a harder target. He just wanted to cover the distance quickly and get to the edge of the wall. In the distance, he could hear the faint hum of helicopters circling the warehouse.

He was nearly at the interface of civilization and nature, the wall forty feet away...twenty...ten. Mitch came to a halt at the edge of the coarse barrier which was nearly two feet thick. He tried to muffle his breath, straining to contain his exhales through his nose, which made him sound like a muzzled bull just before it's released into the rodeo grounds. He scanned the clay soil ahead but didn't see any tracks. Mitch looked for any signs of counter-tracking moves but realized Perry wouldn't have any time to apply such maneuvers. He knelt down and slowly peered around the corner, but did not see any signs of the man or his passage except some crushed grass against the wall, fifty feet away.

He crept a few feet along the other side of the barrier, squinting into the sun to study the disturbance. He noticed that there was a tiny triangle-shaped fracture in the wall, obscured by the undergrowth, just large enough to crawl through. Mitch smelled the musky odor of sweat hanging in the air, confirming Perry was close.

He turned to backpedal from his location and heard the faint sound of crunching grass coming from the other side of the wall by the meadow. Mitch raised his pistol up with his left hand and grabbed a flash-bang grenade off his vest.

"So there goes my plan for shooting you in the back, ole partner," said Perry from the other side.

"You did that back in Arizona when you betrayed me—and your own men."

"Ah, here we go—the dreaded morality tale from you I

was hoping to avoid. The world is a nasty place, Mitch, you know that. You just wanted to keep believing it can be a nice and tidy place with a righteous enough cause."

"Maybe, but at least I have a cause worth fighting for." Mitch could hear Perry creeping towards the corner of the wall while he stood his ground six feet away with his weapon hand extended.

"Give me a break, amigo. You're a fucking lost cause if ever I saw one, showing up at work lookin' like a homeless guy, with an ex-wife who couldn't live with your sorry ass anymore—you've been a cheese-dick since the day I met you." Perry emitted a high-pitched cackle. "Shit, is that what you think that woman sees you in—someone to redeem from his pathetic life?"

Perry was at the edge of the wall, the shadow of his head stretching across the clay soil on Mitch's side. "What happens now, pal? You gonna round the corner and start shooting or should I?" said Perry.

"Why don't we just go at the same time like an old-fashioned duel?"

"Not bad, that's funny. Not a side I saw of you very much, I have to say."

"The only side of yours I want to hear about before I kill you is why—why did you sell out your own country?"

"You wouldn't understand. You seem satisfied with a forty-nine-thousand-dollar-a-year salary and enough beans in your cupboard to get by month-to-month."

"At least I can look in the mirror every day and not hang my head in shame."

Mitch pulled the pin from the flash-bang and then tossed the grenade. As it went over the top of the wall behind Perry, Mitch dove to his left.

With the explosion driving Perry forward, Mitch rolled

on his left shoulder, firing four rounds, two penetrating Perry's shoulder and the rest shattering his shooting arm. The man staggered back, dropping his weapon and crumbling to the ground.

Mitch bolted to his feet and ran over to him, grabbing Perry's pistol. He moved back a few feet near Perry's head, watching as the wounded man's ribs tried to push out a breath as his wounds seeped onto the grass.

"I oughta put you down right now. Leave your body here for the sewer rats."

"Go ahead. I'd do the same if I were in your boots."

"You can go with Ryker when he arrives and carts you off where you'll probably be whacked by one of Ritter's guys for what you know about Aeneid or…"

Mitch removed the magazine from Perry's Sig pistol, stripping out every bullet but one. He slid it back in and tossed the weapon on the ground a foot from Perry's damaged arm.

"Or I can go out Samurai style, is that it—with my honor intact." He slid his hand over the grip of the pistol and began raising it up.

"Something like that," Mitch said, keeping his own pistol aimed at Perry.

Perry slid the weapon up to his temple, looking back at Mitch and then up at the sky. "Goddammit." His trembling hand struggled to steady the barrel as he pulled the trigger, the front of his skull splintering over the espresso-colored clay.

Mitch turned his back and walked a few feet away, his mind reeling from the events of the past two days and the betrayal of someone he had trusted. He heard the footfalls of other men as they trotted across the meadow towards him. He pivoted and saw Ryker in the lead. *Is this really over or has it just begun?*

He wondered how Dev and Anatoly had fared in apprehending Ritter and the terrorists. He would know soon enough. He holstered his Glock and got down on his knees, cupping his hands behind his head as the FBI agents arrived, never imagining he'd be on the receiving end of their charge.

38

Dev clutched Anatoly's lifeless body in her arms in the back seat of the van as they sped along the highway, gaining distance from the warehouse. She felt like she was dead inside—as though the fingers of the grim reaper had plunged into her chest, contemplating removing her heart but then cruelly releasing its grip.

Once they had made it northeast of Anaheim, Petra motioned to pull off along a forested road adjacent to the Chino Hills State Park. Heading back into the woods for a mile, the vehicle stopped beside a small creek. Petra and the other men indicated they would stand watch nearby, giving her time alone to mourn.

Dev had been keeping her anguish padlocked inside in front of the other men but now she wept openly, pleading to go with her father if she couldn't keep him in this world. With all of the mental and physical hardship she had endured in preparation for becoming a warrior, she never knew there would come a day when her being would drown in such sorrow. After what seemed like an hour, her abs cramped from the strain of crying, the flames of grief consuming her parched soul until her tears were exhausted.

She brushed her slender fingers over his bear-like hands, remembering the strength he possessed in the physical realm and his charismatic nature that commanded respect from everyone around the man. Though she had lesser field experience than many of the other staff at her father's company, the reins of command would fall upon her. She gulped in several deep breaths, recalling Anatoly's training, knowing she had to collect herself. She sat up, resting his head gently on the seat and arranging his arms across his chest. Then she covered him with several jackets.

Dev leaned over him one more time, her head lowering, then she felt something deep in her chest begin to burn as the thought of Ritter escaping entered the periphery of her mind. She balled her fists and seethed, the feeling of emptiness inside her filling with rage. The memory of the flash flood she was nearly caught in surfaced and she felt like tearing through everything in her path.

What would happen to Ritter? Would he disappear out of the country, whisked away in his private jet to begin a new life in some foreign land? Would he go into witness protection after snaking his way out of an indictment? Or would his government connections expunge his involvement in the whole undertaking, making him out to be an innocent pawn?

She grit her teeth and smashed her fist against the wall. It wouldn't matter if Ritter tried to elude justice—regardless of where he went or what pains he undertook to begin a new life, Dev would hunt down and destroy the beast. For now, she would have to wait and see what unfolded once the feds had dissected the entire operation between Fareed and Aeneid. She looked out the tinted rear window at the silhouette of cedar trees in the distance, her eyes narrowing. "I will come for you, Nelson Ritter. I will come for you."

After she had recited the mantra a dozen times, she wiped the moist corners of her eyes with her shirt sleeve and then inhaled deeply again, casting open the side door. Dev strode through the woods to where Petra stood and called the other men over. She arched her shoulders back and forced her chin up.

"You all need to disperse and find your way out of the country tonight."

"There was a parking lot I saw a mile back where we can obtain a new vehicle," said Petra.

"Remember the protocols: different airports, different airlines, and different departure times. I will contact the office back home and have them provide cover stories for each of you."

Petra placed his hand on her shoulder while glancing back at the van. "What about Anatoly? He deserves a warrior's burial."

She saw behind Petra a grove of cedar trees beyond the creek. Dev motioned for the men to help her move Anatoly's body, the procession transporting him to the sylvan location. They enclosed him in a crude grave of rocks and each man gave a silent nod to the old warrior. When they were done, Dev moved to the side of the grave and looked at the others, who were lined up side by side in formation. "I know he would be honored by your loyalty but he would want all of you to consider your own safety first. Go now, my brothers. I will take care of things from here."

When the men had dispersed, her disciplined exterior gave way again to the torrent of grief that she'd barely held at bay. She clutched a branch of the cedar tree and removed a palmful of the fragrant sprigs, inhaling their essence.

"Please forgive me for leaving you here away from home. I have little choice, but know that we will see each other again, Poppa."

She placed a handful of cedar sprigs on the rockpile and then gently put the rest in her shirt pocket. Dev pried herself away from the grave and went back to the van. She drove off silently, her shoulders hunched over the steering wheel, heading back to the highway with the image of the creekside resting place in the rearview mirror never seeming to fade from her vision.

39

Two weeks later, outside the federal courthouse in downtown Sacramento, throngs of reporters along with hundreds of spectators stood on the polished granite steps as the single defendant walked down, his limp aided by an ivory-handled cane. Nelson Ritter had a faint grin, his coconut-white teeth showing through his lips as he strode confidently to his curbside limousine. The reporters swarmed around him, thrusting their microphones and cameras in his face. Stopping before the limo door, he adjusted his blue silk necktie and turned to the crowd.

"Mr. Ritter, do you feel that Aeneid was wrongly accused in connection with the thwarted terrorist attacks?" yelled one reporter.

"Sir, is the federal government using your company as a scapegoat for their lack of foresight in handling the situation with assault weapons entering this country illegally?" said a redheaded woman to his right.

He waved his hand for them to be quiet. "Patriotism for this nation has always been my cause and I will continue to push forward with my company's good name. We will have our day in court and the truth behind this fiasco will be known. That is all."

Ritter got inside the limo and sat down, reaching for a carafe of chilled red wine in the open ice chest across from him. His chairside phone rang.

"Nice speech that I just saw on TV," said Monroe. "But take it from me, with all my years in public office, you're better off just nodding politely to the trolls than trying to present the façade of doing damage control."

"Relax, I gave the guppies a few morsels to blog about for the next week. Besides, I've sat stone-faced through this inane hearing for three days now and I felt like saying a few words on my behalf."

"The whole matter should be waylaid by the end of the week and your role in the matter resolved, according to my contacts."

"Ah, you're too kind. Are you sure there's a politician inside you?" He chuckled, taking a sip of wine from his silver goblet. "Are we still going to meet on Saturday to discuss moving ahead with Plan B?"

"Yes, the usual location. Have your men secure the area again—and Nelson, try and keep your trap shut for the cameras until then."

40

THE ASPEN LOGS in the fireplace at Thomas Monroe's Tahoe chalet sputtered out a succession of hisses as he and Nelson Ritter sat on the elephant-hide recliners, sipping brandy and chuckling.

"And then the judge says, 'Agent Mitchell Kearns, your testimony is inconclusive. You are still under investigation by your own department which, by the way, is a federal agency,'" Nelson Ritter said while trying to choke down another swig of whiskey in between bouts of laughter. "And the best part is that the woman, Leitner...Sanchez...whoever the fuck she is...she disappeared, leaving Kearns to hang in the wind."

Monroe nodded and smiled. "That judge couldn't be bought off in the beginning so we had to use some incriminating photos of his youngest daughter at college that one of my men obtained with the help of—uhm, what do the kids call 'em these days...ah...roofies."

Two guards in three-piece suits stood by the front and rear doors, resembling statues except for the automatic weapons slung about their shoulders. Three more men were doing foot patrols along the spruce-lined forest surrounding the luxurious A-frame.

"The FBI is facing a possible scandal if I have my say and the relations with the Israelis could—well, you know—become strained between our two governments," continued Monroe, the shot of liquid bravery infusing him with more bravado than he was accustomed to.

"There's still the matter of Kearns. He's the reason this whole goddamned mess got as far as it did. If he hadn't helped that woman and eluded my man Drake in the desert this whole fucking thing could've ended without incident. Months in the planning to get this Fareed fellow to sign on with the whole religious agenda. Now the Caspian Sea operation is delayed."

"It shouldn't be too hard to find another loyal extremist to get on board with a different cause in another region of our country or even Europe. As for Kearns, I'll see to it he has a horseback riding accident somewhere on that ranch. Shit—why not torch that entire place and finish what he started?"

Nelson raised his glass in a toast. "I'll have to get another shell corporation created to cloak any movement now that Aeneid is under the spotlight. I hope you can still help with covering the digital trail."

Monroe shook his head, laughing and pouring himself another drink. "Cheers, my good man." Raising the golden elixir to his lips, he heard the crackling of wood to his right, realizing it was opposite the fireplace and a higher pitch than the burning aspen. The ear-splitting sound had emanated from the guard by the rear door as his cheekbone split open from a single round, the man collapsing to the oaken floor. Before Monroe could stand, another round sliced through the glass in his own hand, spraying shards into his face. He fell back into the recliner and began yelling as the second guard was cut down by two rounds that pierced his neck.

"We've gotta get out of here," said Monroe, reaching for the walkie-talkie on the mahogany table beside him. "Guards—guards, get up here," he yelled while flopping to the floor on his belly.

"They're dead, you fool," muttered Nelson. "If these two are already gone, then you can bet we're all alone."

"Those fucking Iranians. It has to be them...but how did they find us up here?" said Monroe, his fear rising like tendrils of smoke.

Nelson slithered towards his briefcase to extract a pistol. Just as he reached it, he felt the sting of his kneecap explode, as if a mighty hammer had been driven from above. He recoiled into the couch, his body going fetal as he screamed and looked into the face of Dev Leitner walking through the back door.

She was dressed in black, with inky streaks running diagonally across her face, her brown eyes magnified by the firelight as if they were conspiring to consume the cabin. Dev turned towards Monroe and stepped on his injured hand as he tried to reach for an iron poker near the hearth.

"I really thought about making this look like an accident. I really did," she said. "I had a couple of well-planned scenarios but I just had to be sure that neither of you sons of bitches got away by some stroke of luck." She stood over Nelson, her pistol steady. "Some people are opposed to violence...and they are protected by those who are not." She fired a round into Nelson's head, which blew apart and sent rivulets of blood into the fire.

Monroe's wailing increased as she moved closer, and he simpered like a pig set upon by wild dogs. "Please, it doesn't have to end this way. I have considerable power at the DOD that could be to your benefit."

She removed a bronze dagger from her vest and leaned over, driving it into his chest. "Time to pass that on to your successor," she said, slamming Fareed's old blade into the plump man's chest a second time. Dev stared into Monroe's glassy eyes then stood up and knocked the bottle of brandy off the table towards the fireplace. Its contents quickly became engulfed with flames that spread along the oaken floorboards towards the two splayed figures.

As the chalet became consumed by the intense fire, she hurried to the back door, stepping over the deceased bodyguard and trotting down the back stairs of the porch. As Dev slipped into the spruce forest, the A-frame behind her was illuminated blood-orange as she strode over the soft matting of old conifer needles.

She felt the rage born of loss flow over her as if the conflagration was emanating from her body. The falling snow covered her tracks and dampened the sound of the forest until even the crackling of consumed timber behind her faded. Dev walked another two miles to a narrow dirt road, below which the jeep she stole earlier was concealed in a thicket. She got in the vehicle and headed down the mountain, towards the pitch-black horizon, the flames on the mountainside stabbing upward into the clutches of the sky.

41

THREE WEEKS LATER, after the trial had been dismissed and Aeneid's doors shuttered, Mitch found himself adrift. His involvement in the whole affair had been shown to be instrumental in thwarting the terrorist attack. Ryker had gone to considerable effort to make sure Mitch's record was expunged of any local and federal law enforcement misdeeds.

Perry was officially listed as KIA in the line of duty while his records, files, and personal life were being investigated by a bureau panel for his connections to Aeneid and other potential sources associated to information he leaked.

Publicly, blame was cast upon Fareed and his radicalized group of disillusioned friends, his previous visit to Yemen cementing his lone-wolf plot with arms dealer Gamal, who had apparently committed suicide afterwards. This story allowed the national outrage to be channeled enough to divert attention from the mess created with Monroe's and Aeneid's involvement.

The usual statements of deniability were issued between the U.S. and Israeli government while keeping the matter of

Monroe's nebulous undertakings out of the media spotlight. All of the credit was directed at Bureau Chief Evan Ryker, who was in the spotlight, relaying the FBI's investigative work that led to thwarting the attack.

After learning of the Leitners' involvement through Mitch and with the state department looking for an excuse to patch up strained relations with Israel, Dev's participation was never officially recognized as the only witnesses to her involvement were Perry and Ritter. Her face was removed from the FBI's Most Wanted list after Perry's meddling was uncovered.

A few days after returning to Arizona, Mitch headed straight to his friend's ranch, where he spent time building a new bunkhouse and doing a lot of campfire cooking for the crew. He stayed in a small twelve-by-sixteen cabin near the horse pasture, enjoying catching up on whittling, reading, and tracking animals.

Early one morning, when the purple finches were singing in the cottonwood tree above his rustic abode, he heard the ranch hands near the entrance gate talking to someone who had just driven up. A few minutes later, a red Prius rolled down the hill. Dev Leitner had never looked as stunning as when she stepped into the sunlight. She wore a red tank-top which hung slightly over her jeans.

She looked over at the framework of the bunkhouse and then made a beeline for Mitch. He stood up and walked down the steps of his tiny porch, meeting her halfway.

"The new place is coming along nicely, though not as rustic as the original."

"A few years in this weather and it'll look as old as the first one."

He tossed the stick that he'd been whittling on the ground and put away his folding knife. "You know a funny thing happened—about two weeks ago, the owner of the ranch gets an anonymous check in the mail. Says it's from an overseas company out of Tel Aviv that donates to various causes and that he should apply it towards renovation of a historic structure on his property."

"Huh...wow...isn't the mail wonderful. I mean, you can just get those kind of surprises through your mailbox."

"Yeah, I told him he oughta blow most of the money on beer and new saddles but he managed to save a few pennies for nails and lumber."

She folded her arms across her chest, giving him a fierce stare that then turned into a grin. "Mitch Kearns, you're sounding more like a cowboy than a federal agent with each sentence. You sure you're the same guy I met a month ago?"

He arched his back up to the blue sky and stretched his arms out to his sides. "I'm back home where I belong, at least for now. Got my old job back with the feds if I want it but I'm still thinking about that one. What brings you out to these parts again?" he said jokingly while looking up at the ridgeline, half-wondering if there were any surprises.

They walked up to the porch, where he offered her his only chair while he leaned against the railing. For the next few hours they spoke about the trial, the FBI, Anatoly, and geopolitics in Turkmenistan.

"It looks like your father's legacy will remain intact. He's done a lot to ensure their way of life will continue and I know he'd be damn proud of you." Mitch lowered his head, thinking of the warrior philanthropist and what he had risked for so many over the years while remaining in the shadows. "He was a helluva guy. Tonight we'll have a campfire and meal in his honor."

"I wish I could but I should be going. I only drove out here to say goodbye and to—" She paused, looking up at him and smiling. "To thank you for putting so much on the line for me when you could've looked the other way."

"My pleasure, ma'am," he said, tilting the brim of his white cowboy hat.

He got up and went inside his cabin, removing two cold beers from his cooler and returning. He removed the lids and then handed her one. "We have to at least give a cowboy salute to the heavens above for not getting rained on this time."

"I'll drink to that," she said, standing up.

He took a long swig and then leaned against the wall. "You know that was pretty shocking what happened in Lake Tahoe to the assistant sec-def, Ritter, and his entourage. Don't know if you read about it in the papers?"

She just raised an eyebrow and continued fixing her gaze upon the ground ahead. "Pretty shocking alright."

"Some Iranians connected to Fareed and his guys—they think, though that's not official." He strolled over to her, reaching a hand up to the porch rafter and staring out at the cottonwood trees. "Gotta be careful when you wander into the backcountry." He tilted his head towards her, looking into her brown eyes. "Know what I mean?"

She just smiled and tucked a thumb into her belt loop. "Yep."

"Sure you can't stick around? We could do some horseback riding and run across a few mesas for fun."

"Sounds swell—but, you know, I should be getting back home." She walked around the front porch, the railing between them, resting her hands on the cracked wood. She wanted to stay—to get to know him better without the chaos of what they had endured—but she felt herself closing up inside. She needed to get back to Israel, to her mother, to her father's company, and to piece together her fractured heart.

"You never can tell when I'll be back in these parts though—hopefully on more pleasant business."

He extended his hand over hers, caressing her wrist with his thumb. "Until then, I hope you'll remember us rednecks."

She grinned and tossed her head back, flinging her raven hair over her shoulder. "Shouldn't take too much effort." Dev turned and walked to her car, climbing inside and pausing to wave one last time before driving up the dusty road.

42

A MONTH LATER, after all of the debriefings had finished and Mitch had used up the rest of his considerable vacation days, he walked along the battleship-gray carpeting on the second floor of the FBI building in downtown Phoenix, striding by familiar faces who cast lilted smiles of recognition. He didn't care—there were few people there that he desired to work with and he wondered how he had pressed on in that stifling job for so long.

Mitch walked into his office and began packing his items. He wasn't sure what was next for him but it had to involve being outdoors and entail travel. No sitting still or checking endless emails or hunting two-bit fugitives. Maybe he'd find work on a ranch for part of the year. Then again, he knew that was back-breaking work best suited towards a younger man with a more pliable body.

"Leaving without a farewell?" said Ryker, who was standing in the doorway. "So, that's it—unravel a terrorist cell and internal corruption and it's time to hang your hat up."

Mitch had come to respect the man, though he still

didn't like him very much. They were just too opposite in every way. "Thought I'd take some time off and go on a long horse-packing trip, maybe up on Apache land for a while."

"I can still use you if you ever get tired of roastin' corn over da campfire," he said in a weak attempt at a cowboy accent that sounded more like someone from Georgia.

"Thanks. I think my next job will involve a little less bureaucracy and suit-wearing."

Ryker walked forward and extended his hand. After they had shaken, the bureau chief turned away then came to a halt. "Almost forgot—this was dropped off at the front desk below," he said, reaching into his jacket pocket and removing an envelope. "It's already been scanned so no surprises inside."

Ryker closed the door. Mitch tapped the envelope against his palm, noticing it was post-marked as international mail. He removed his small folder and slit open the edge. The sentences that followed were penned in beautiful blue cursive.

Mitch,

It seems the Israeli military wants to revive their combat tracking program! They are looking for independent contractors to provide training and your name may have made it into their queue. Tel Aviv is lovely in the fall. What do you say, cowboy?

Dev

He put the letter down and walked over to the tinted window. Mitch stood with his hands on his hips, gazing at the cobalt desert sky and tracing it down to where it melted into the horizon.

What indeed?

FREE MITCH KEARNS SHORT STORY

Thank you for reading this book! There are 12 more books in the Mitch Kearns Combat Tracker Series and you can join Mitch & Dev in their further adventures in the second book, *Counter Strike*, now available on Amazon.

You can also obtain a FREE Mitch Kearns' short story, *Blood on the Mesa*, by joining my email list. This prequel follows Mitch on an FBI case, tracking down a murderer and stolen prehistoric artifacts in the desert near Winslow, Arizona in the days leading up to *Dead In Their Tracks*. You can pick up a copy at jtsawyer.com

ABOUT THE AUTHOR

Before becoming a fulltime writer, JT made his living teaching survival courses for the military special operations community, Department of Homeland Security, US Marshals, FAA, and other federal agencies throughout the US. He also served as a consultant for the film *Into the Wild* and has been a longtime freelance writer for magazines like Outside, Backpacker, and Backwoods Survival. Nowadays, JT prefers having a roof over his head and placing his fictional characters in dire situations in the urban wilds in his thriller and post-apocalyptic books. He lives in Colorado Springs, CO.

SEARCH AND DESTROY: A CAL SHEPARD BLACK-OPS THRILLER

The CIA created him. Treachery unleashed him.

Cal Shepard was trained by the government to be a hunter of other assassins. He's the tip of the spear in the war on terror and a master of tradecraft after 16 years in black-ops.

When he's assigned to be a consultant for the Burke Corporation, a US defense firm creating a software-targeting database of terrorist threats, he thinks his time in the field is over. Days before the database is supposed to go live, he is framed for murder and becomes the target of a nationwide manhunt.

But he's not about to disappear....not without exacting revenge.

With an FBI task force on his trail and a group of hired guns needing to take him down before he can uncover the truth, Shepard realizes that the network of corruption extends to the upper echelons of the government. Applying his well-honed skills from years of search & destroy missions, Shepard takes the fight to the enemy, methodically hunting down those responsible and dispensing his own brand of justice.

Available in both print and digital versions on Amazon

POST-APOCALYPTIC THRILLERS BY JT SAWYER

The Emergence Series, Volumes 1-8
First Wave Series
Until Morning Comes Series
Hell Week I & II
Horror From Below Series

NON-FICTION SURVIVAL BOOKS BY TONY NESTER (AKA JT SAWYER)

Knife-Only Survival
Bushcraft Tips & Tools
Bug-Out Gear for Travelers
When the Grid Goes Down
Survival Gear You Can Live With
A Vehicle Survival Kit You Can Live With
Life Under Open Skies: Adventures in Bushcraft

Made in United States
North Haven, CT
16 July 2023